"That's right, Celty! You figured it out! Incredible, Celty—we are truly of one mind and spirit! Our hearts are connected! What's yours is yours, and what's mine is yours, except for one thing: Your *heart* is mine!"

"...You're usually so calm and collected. Why do you freak out about Yahiro like this?"

VOLUME 3

Ryohgo Narita
ILLUSTRATION BY Suzuhito Yasuda

NEW YORK

Durarara!! SH, Vol. 3
Ryohgo Narita

Translation by Stephen Paul
Yen On edition edited by Carly Smith & Yen Press Editorial
Cover art by Suzuhito Yasuda

DURARARA!! SH Vol. 3
©RYOHGO NARITA 2015
Edited by Dengeki Bunko
First published in Japan in 2015 by KADOKAWA CORPORATION, Tokyo.
English translation rights arranged with KADOKAWA CORPORATION, Tokyo,
through TUTTLE-MORI AGENCY, INC., Tokyo.

English translation © 2022 by Yen Press, LLC

Yen On
150 West 30th Street, 19th Floor
New York, NY 10001

Visit us at yenpress.com
facebook.com/yenpress
twitter.com/yenpress
yenpress.tumblr.com
instagram.com/yenpress

First Yen On Edition: March 2022

Yen On is an imprint of Yen Press, LLC.
The Yen On name and logo are trademarks of Yen Press, LLC.

Library of Congress Cataloging-in-Publication Data
Names: Narita, Ryōgo, 1980– author. | Yasuda, Suzuhito, illustrator. |
Paul, Stephen (Translator), translator.
Title: Durarara!! SH / Ryohgo Narita ; illustration by Suzuhito Yasuda ;
translation by Stephen Paul.
Other titles: Durarara!! (Light novel). English
Description: First Yen On edition. | New York : Yen On, 2021.
Identifiers: LCCN 2021009783 | ISBN 9781975322779
(v. 1 ; trade paperback) | ISBN 9781975323462 (v. 2 ; trade paperback) |
ISBN 9781975323486 (v. 3 ; trade paperback)
Subjects: CYAC: Fantasy. | Tokyo (Japan)—Fiction.
Classification: LCC PZ7.1.N37 Dur 2021 | DDC [Fic]—dc23
LC record available at https://lccn.loc.gov/2021009783

ISBNs: 978-1-9753-2348-6 (paperback)
         978-1-9753-2349-3 (ebook)

1 3 5 7 9 10 8 6 4 2

WOR

Printed in the United States of America

The Words of an Info Broker

I love humanity.

I've said as much many times in my life.
I. Love. People. It's true.
It might sound like a trite statement, but I've never shied away from saying it. In fact, my love for humanity is so true that I don't know any other way to say it.
I suppose if you wanted, you could call me a *fan*.
Yes, I'm a fan of humanity.

"I'm a fan of man!"
…Have you ever heard that line before? It's from a famous movie.
A master actor plays the Devil, and he says it to a pious young human man to tempt him. "I'm a humanist," he says.
I'm not the Devil, of course. I'm just a normal human being without so much as a single supernatural power. But I am one of humanity's biggest fans.
The thing is, all people are fans of man. Don't you agree?
Fan, of course, being short for *fanatic*. Human beings are constantly fanatical for their fellows.
Some people would deny that, of course. It's only natural. That's what you *want* from people.
Some people can't help but detest humanity, and others say they have no interest. Funny thing about that is—both hatred and indifference are types of fanaticism.
In Japanese, the word *fanaticism* is written with the kanji for *heat* and *madness*. Do you see where I'm going with this?

To go mad over heat itself. To go mad when heat is applied.

And for *one's own heat to go mad*. All these interpretations are valid.

The heat one feels for humanity going out of control—that's me. Overheating and falling in love with humanity itself.

Others become too cold and detest humanity instead.

Those who take on neither heat nor cold, maintaining perfect equilibrium no matter what happens around them, are also experiencing an abnormality in calibration.

Personality can also be shaped by things outside of humanity... Say, being struck by the majesty of nature or undergoing a terrifying wild animal attack.

However, only humans can alter the enthusiasm they feel toward humanity as a whole.

Let's say you've got someone who says, *Everyone around me is such a tired, predictable bore. They don't inspire anything in me.*

If you ask me, that person's feeling the influence from humanity stronger than anyone. After all, he's receiving the emotion of boredom from others. It's much harder than you'd think for your emotions to be perpetually changing—did you know that?

Let's say you've hated a type of food since you were a child. If someone told you to simply get over it and change your opinion, it wouldn't be that easy, would it?

It takes a vast amount of energy to constantly provide a human being with the feeling of boredom. Just think about it.

Sure, looking at rocks is boring. That's because rocks don't move. Human beings are constantly moving, though. The more you observe them, the more often you're likely to see a new side of them.

Therefore, someone has to actively try to feel consistently bored.

Does that sound facetious to you?

Well, of course. I'm using facetious logic. The truth is, I don't care what anyone else says. The important thing is, what about yourself?

I love humanity. Yes, I love it deeply.

I've been saying that for years, which is why I think humanity should be allowed to love me, too.

Mutual love with all humanity—what a wonderful thing.

It could be love that gently envelops me.

It could be love that virulently insults me.

It could even be love that ignores me.

Do you really think love doesn't have a shape? Really?

Love has a shape; it's just always changing.

I want to prove that to everyone.

Ultimately, I want to connect with people—that's all. I want to move around as many people as possible, stirring up the world like a sticky batch of natto, creating tendrils between people that stretch and stretch and tangle up with one another.

That desire made me the man I am today.

It's a good thing to be fanatical toward each other. *Very* good.

Even if the law and society are against it, I will accept you.

So don't worry—go wild out there.

Love others; hate others; be perfectly indifferent.

Each of those choices is equal, and each has great value.

PROLOGUE

PROLOGUE
Let's Take One Giant Leap

It wandered the city without a real destination in mind.

One more step.

Just for that single, meager step that would change itself.

If it did so of its own accord, it could step over that pale, little line created by its own brain.

Or perhaps—stomp directly on it.

♂♀

Tokyo—midnight

"Huh? Hey, look at that, over there."

Night had long since fallen in the twenty-three wards of Tokyo.

Even in the middle of the big city, darkness still lurked in the corners.

An adult couple was making their way down a path to the park when both parties just so happened to encounter *it*, walking along the edge of the street.

"Oh…? What is that?"

"Look, it's, um… What's it called? You know, the one from the zombie movie or whatever."

"Oh! Oh! Oh! The Ikebukuro one!"

On the otherwise empty street, they were talking about a figure wearing full-body pajamas designed in a way to look like an owl, with a special hood that could fit entirely over the head.

The unknown entity inside was wearing the hood, which completely covered their face, aside from their eyes.

As the two walked past the figure, assuming it was dressed up as a character from a movie, they wondered to each other, "What's it called again? Dark something or other. It's the bad guy, the evil zombie."

"So I guess that's a cosplayer?"

It wasn't unprecedented for people in Ikebukuro to walk around dressed as fictional characters or to wear *kigurumi* pajamas fashioned after bunnies or cats. There didn't even need to be some particular event going on; you could see them now and then on an ordinary day on Sunshine 60 Street.

The couple assumed this person was someone on the way home from a party or perhaps filming some kind of attempt at a viral video.

They were quickly proved wrong.

The first to be shocked was the man, but the first to notice the anomaly was the woman.

That was because it was the man who felt a shock in his head and fell unconscious before he could register that something was wrong.

"Huh...? Wha...? Eh?"

At the same moment she heard a dull thud, the woman witnessed the man topple forward.

She also witnessed the pajama-clad person practically teleport behind the man as they clutched a hammer wrapped in several layers of bandages.

"..."

Silently, the figure in the *kigurumi* lifted the hammer overhead.

"Wait... Stoppp!"

The woman screamed and tried to run away, but she tripped over the fallen body of her boyfriend. She scrambled away, trying to stand again, and looked back at the figure of her attacker.

I remember now.

Her entire body felt like it was paralyzed, making the flow of time slow to a crawl. Within that headspace she recalled, with crystal clarity, exactly what those costume pajamas were based upon.

That's right. I remember. It wasn't a movie; it was an anime or a manga of some kind.

The woman worked at a hostess club in Ikebukuro. A younger hostess coworker who had recently been hired was a fan of that series. She often brought anime merchandise and manga volumes into the break room in the back.

A few years ago, the series was adapted into a live-action film to moderate success, so the woman had learned the general gist of the plot as a topic of conversation with the club's clients.

She thought it would be worth knowing about because the original anime took place in a city based on Ikebukuro, where the hostess club was, and most of the locations in the movie were shot in the area.

And the name was…

Despite her struggle to get away, the woman's mind was occupied with recalling this totally inconsequential piece of information as if it was the key to her escape.

But while she might have been hoping that learning the name of her mysterious attacker would ease her fear, ultimately no one aside from her could have said what was in her chaotic thoughts.

That's it! I remember! I remember!

"Da… D-Da…Dark Owl—*brgah!*"

The name left her lips at the same moment the hammer came down upon her head.

♂♀

The next day

"We have new information pertaining to the random street attack that occurred in Tokyo.

*　　　*　　　*

"*According to a statement given by a victim once she came to, the attacker was wearing a costume resembling an animated character. The police are seeking further eyewitnesses...*"

♂♀

Ten days later

"*There has been another person attacked on the street in Tokyo. A man in Toshima Ward was bludgeoned by another man from behind. His injuries are serious enough to take an estimated two months to heal...*

"*Based on what officials believe to be the weapon, corroborated by eyewitness information, police think it is possible this attack was carried out by the same perpetrator of an attack earlier this month...*

"*Eyewitness accounts described the attacker as being dressed like a character out of a movie.*"

♂♀

Fifteen days later

"*We have an update on the string of attacks in Tokyo. There has been another incident.*

"*The attacker was seen disguised as a character from a popular anime that was turned into a movie this February...*

"*That puts the total number of victims at seven.*

"*Maou Publishing, the publisher of the original manga the anime is based upon, said in a statement, 'We pray for a swift recovery for the victims of these attacks. We are outraged by these incidents and ask the police to resolve these events as soon as possible.'*"

"*In a previous news segment, we mistakenly described Maou as being* the publisher of the 'original manga.' To be accurate, the manga is not the original work but an adaptation. We regret any confusion our mistake might have caused."

♂♀

Twenty days later

"The franchise in question is Owl of the Peeping Dead, often abbreviated as OPD. It's the multimedia product of a creative collective called Walking with Wizards, or WWW, and it's the animation in particular that has attracted quite a following.

"Joining us as an expert for this segment will be the anime columnist and writer Jackson Ushidaira."

"Thank you for having me."

"Mr. Ushidaira, this is the piece of merchandise the attacker has been seen wearing, a set of pajamas called Dark Owl. Is this kigurumi set meant to resemble the character in the story?"

"Actually, it's less that it resembles the character and more that the character wears a set of costume pajamas that look exactly like these. In fact, their face has never been revealed in the story, so to the fans, the kigurumi might as well be the character itself."

"Thank you for that explanation. The series is quite a hit, having a successful live-action film and popularity abroad. However, it must be noted that even before these attacks began, the anime, manga, and live-action versions were controversial for their violent content..."

♂♀

Ikebukuro West Gate Park—private room of Pasela Karaoke

"It's not OPD's fault! OPD is innocent!" protested a narrow-eyed man, waving his arms frantically. "Yes, it's the most violent among all the adult-oriented manga in Maou's stable, but it's only depicted *against* the zombies; plus, the whole point of the story is that it's about a man who gets killed and turned into a zombie but retains his mind and practices strict nonviolence against the human beings who are trying to kill him! Whoever's using a hammer to attack humans doesn't understand the *slightest bit* of the spirit of the work!"

The woman sitting next to him calmly opined, "Maybe they were inspired by the villain. Supposedly, the attacker was dressed as the Dark Owl."

"Damn… Well, it's true that the Dark Owl plots to take over Ike-bukuro using zombified bodies…but that's a villain! I mean, if you're gonna practice evil and say you're becoming the villain, then you were *already* messed up from the start! You can't blame the manga for influencing you! Anyway, my point is…*OPD* is awesome!"

The reaction of the person sitting across from the passionate, narrow-eyed man was almost diametrically opposite. He was wearing a Raira Academy uniform, and his name was Yahiro Mizuchi.

"Uh-huh."

His reaction wasn't meant to insult the man's enthusiasm in any way; it was pure bafflement. It meant, *I don't know how I should react to this, so I might as well murmur in understanding.*

Yahiro didn't have any particular feeling toward the manga the man was preaching about, but he wasn't going to ignore the story, either. He just listened closely.

This was Yahiro's first time meeting this eccentric man.

Typically, this was the sort of scenario in which you would ignore what the man was saying, but Yahiro listened as intently as though he were in class, receiving a lecture.

Why was a high schooler like him listening to this unfamiliar man's complaints in a karaoke room?

It was his job.

Simple as that.
It was part of the job he'd decided to undertake just minutes earlier.

CHAPTER
1

CHAPTER 1
Welcome to Snake Hands

Late April, Sixtieth Floor Street, Ikebukuro

"Snake Hands? What is that? Some kind of rip-off of Tokyu Hands?"

Golden Week was rapidly approaching in Ikebukuro.

In a fairly crowded restaurant in the evening, a teenager was discussing the latest rumors. They were the typical ones that any teenager would talk about, the sort of conversation you would completely forget about a few hours later. But then a strange name popped up.

"Oh, you mean the guy they say is the boyfriend of the Headless Rider?"

"Yeah, apparently he's super messed up. Remember how there was that big fake group kidnapping a while back? Apparently, he was involved with that."

"Involved...like how?"

"Dunno. The stories also say he wiped out a motorcycle gang or yakuza mob all on his own..."

One person among the coed group paused and changed the course of the topic. "Fake kidnapping, motorcycle gangs? What are you talking about? That was all a setup by some crazed fan of the Headless Rider, wasn't it?"

"That doesn't line up with what I know."

"It doesn't? How so?"

"From what I've heard, Snake Hands is just an odd jobs group in Ikebukuro."

"Odd jobs? What's that?"

The boys laughed; it didn't seem to match their preconception of the Headless Rider in any way.

"Oh, it's like you can get to them from ads on some website somewhere. They do all kinds of stuff for people around Ikebukuro."

"Will they tidy up your room?"

"No, it's not like chores and errands. It's more like…I dunno, moderating fights? Bodyguard services if you're involved in something dangerous? That sort of thing."

"What sort of thing is that?"

"Does that sound scary to you, too? Now, that's something that sounds like it would get you involved with shady underbelly types," said a girl, etching an invisible scar on her cheek.

The first boy to bring it up said, "Like I said, it's just a story. Nobody would actually go online and pay for help from some weird website, you know?"

"I dunno—people will fall for anything."

"That's hilarious."

"Anyway, did you buy the new Ruri Hijiribe song?"

"Yeah, it's so good."

"_____"

"____"

And just like that, the rumor vanished, evolving into a different story.

The students gradually finished their uneventful meal and got up to leave.

But the boy sitting at a table nearby, Yahiro Mizuchi, could not get the name Snake Hands out of his head.

"…"

"What's wrong, Yahiro?" asked a classmate sitting across from him, Himeka Tatsugami. That brought him back to his senses.

Sitting next to him was a green-haired boy, Kuon Kotonami, who teased, "What's up? Is sitting in the presence of girls making you uncharacteristically nervous?"

"You think so? Was I nervous?" Yahiro asked.

Kuon sighed. "Why would you take that question seriously? Look, Himeka's fine because she's used to how unsocial you are, but Akane's clearly got no idea how to react to this."

He was looking across the table at Akane Awakusu, a girl wearing the uniform of a local middle school.

"Oh, I'm fine," she said, bowing. "I'm sorry."

Yahiro bowed back to her. "No, *I'm* sorry. If Kuon's bringing it up, then I must be acting weird."

"No, it's fine. It's nothing. I'm sorry."

"No, it's my bad."

Kuon watched the two bowing and apologizing to each other until he couldn't take it anymore. "How long are you two gonna do that?!"

"Oh, sorry, Kuon."

"I—I'm sorry about that…"

"Stop! This conversation is over! *The! End!* No more apologizing!"

Himeka, too, recognized that this shtick could go on forever, so she led the change in topic. "Anyway, I'm glad that your schoolmate came back safe and sound, Akane."

The girl agreed enthusiastically. "Yeah!"

Akane's schoolmate was an older girl who'd gone missing about two weeks ago, supposedly kidnapped by the Headless Rider. Once it was revealed that the kidnapping was fake, she soon came back safely.

The incident got the news shows and Internet all abuzz for a day or two, but when nobody turned out to be dead and it was just a number of orchestrated runaways, the story went from being tantalizing to being characterized as a "misleading hoax to get a rise out of people." The attention of the city turned to the street attacks next.

"Amazing how things just get right back to normal," Yahiro said.

"The teacher really scolded her, and everyone else had stuff to say, too…but mostly, they're acting like she just ditched school for a week…," Akane said.

"True… A faked kidnapping sounds dramatic, but to middle schoolers, it's basically just ditching school, huh? It's weird—for having involved so many sides, that story sure got wiped out fast by the street attacks," Kuon said.

"It's better that way," Yahiro noted. "I'm glad it didn't turn into a much bigger controversy."

"Uh...I mean, I'm not saying I *wanted* it to be a controversy, ya know?" the green-haired boy protested, no doubt because Himeka was a family member of some of the people involved in the fakery.

Akane's schoolmate was Himeka's younger sister. And Himeka's *older* sister was centrally involved in the faked group kidnapping, too.

Yahiro turned back to Himeka. "I'm glad it sounds like your big sister's going to be out of the hospital soon."

"Yes... Apparently, they'll make an exception to let her go back to work, too," Himeka said.

"Oh, I see," Yahiro said.

"Wait, really?" Kuon exclaimed.

Himeka explained, "The magazine she works for wants to print a special issue about the event. So what better scoop than having an exclusive account from someone involved?"

Yahiro tilted his head. "But won't people assume that the magazine set up the whole thing to sell a story?"

"She works for the kind of magazine that doesn't care about that..."

"Damn, that's crazy," marveled Kuon, twirling the straw in his cream soda.

Meanwhile, Yahiro grinned happily. "Still, I'm happy for you. You get to be back with your sisters at home again."

"Hmm, I guess so."

The names of Himeka's sisters hadn't been reported in the media, so it didn't seem like anyone was talking about her at school.

Yahiro was relieved about that, but he was pleased about something else, too. "You seem happier than before, Himeka."

"...Do I really?"

"Aren't you?"

"...I suppose I am."

Exhausted by this introverted excuse for a conversation, Kuon flailed his arms around dramatically. "What is wrong with you people?! I'll repeat myself: What's wrong with you?!"

Without batting an eye, Himeka asked, "What's the matter, Kotonami?"

"Huh? Did I say something wrong?" Yahiro wondered aloud, self-conscious.

Kuon scratched his head. "Ugh! Honestly! You both talk like robots!

Seriously, you're both teenagers bursting with vitality! Can't you get into some spicier topics?!"

"Are you forgetting there's a younger girl listening in?" Himeka glanced at Akane.

Akane didn't seem to be bothered by Kuon's suggestion; in fact, she was staring eagerly at Himeka and Yahiro, hoping they would continue.

Feeling left out, Kuon frustratedly stirred the cream soda with his spoon and grumbled to Yahiro, "Say, when did you switch from calling her Tatsugami to Himeka? You makin' a move? You are, aren't you? Let me guess: You like her! What a dork!"

He moved on from his childish rant by slurping down the melted mix of ice cream and soda through his straw.

Yahiro answered him anyway. "I mean, if the options are like and don't like, then of course I like her. Himeka's really pretty, and she's super nice."

"......"

"......"

Kuon stared at him, his cheek twitching. Akane had turned a deep, panicked red and was shooting glances at Himeka.

As for Himeka, her expression did not change the tiniest bit. "I don't hate you, either, but in terms of relationships, I'd say it's not at that kind of stage, and it's not something you should decide on the spot anyway."

Yahiro nodded immediately. "Yeah, you're right. Sorry for being weird."

"You don't need to apologize for that."

A red-faced Akane listened to them with obvious confusion, while Kuon scowled bitterly. He repeated, "Ugh, what is wrong with you?! Once again, what's *wrong* with you people?!"

Once the furor died down and Kuon finished his cream soda, he made a big show about changing the topic.

"Man, the world's so violent these days, you know? Like I said, everyone's talking about the street attacks. Now that it's happened a few times, people are saying it's the 'return of the street slasher' and everything."

"Street slasher..."

"Oh, you don't know, Yahiro? Like two years ago, there was this string of slashing incidents on the streets."

"I mean, I heard stories about it."

When doing research on Ikebukuro, he had spotted talk about the Night of the Ripper.

Some people speculated that it had something to do with the street gangs at the time, like the Dollars and Yellow Scarves, but ultimately the string of events simply fizzled out without a conclusive answer on the culprit.

"But the attacker they're talking about on the news now uses a hammer, right? So it's probably not the same person doing it again, I assume," Yahiro said.

"We don't know that. Maybe the guy just felt like a change of weapons. I could imagine they got bored with all the blood and became obsessed with the physical sensation of bludgeoning instead," Himeka said quite matter-of-factly for such violent content.

Yahiro murmured and nodded.

Once she was done with her salt-grilled mackerel meal, Himeka watched Yahiro chow down on his fluffy pancakes and said, "Well, the street attacker is one thing, but we're dealing with someone even more violent, aren't we?"

"Huh? Who? The Headless Rider?" asked Yahiro, fork in hand.

After a few moments of silence, Akane suddenly gasped with realization. "Y-you mean me? I'm sorry..."

Of all people, Akane herself was most conscious of the fact that being the granddaughter of the Awakusu-kai chairman made her a very dangerous person to interact with, hence her apology.

"No, I'm not talking about you, Akane. Sorry to make you feel bad," Himeka apologized back. Then she clarified, "No...I was talking about you, Kotonami."

"Huh?! *Me?!*" Kuon exclaimed, feigning great shock.

She asked, "What is Snake Hands?"

"!" It was Yahiro who reacted. He stopped eating his pancakes and stared at the boy sitting next to him.

Kuon looked up at the ceiling and whistled very unconvincingly. "Whatever do you mean? Are you talking about that guy the people at the other table were talking about? I'm thinking it's probably a nickname for the boyfriend of the Headless Rider, the one from that recent kerfuffle."

"Don't play stupid," Himeka said flatly. She pulled out her smartphone and showed him the screen. Yahiro craned his neck to look at it, too.

The screen displayed the following message.

We'll solve your Ikebukuro problems.
Missing persons, revenge against bullies, personal protection: We do everything!

> *Snake Hands, an Ikebukuro mutual aid group*

That was all that was written on the page. Nothing about actual job conditions, payment, or even a means of contact. There was nothing in there that would dissuade someone from assuming it was just a prank message.

"What is that...? Seems like a weird web page," Kuon said, laughing it off.

But Himeka was determined. "It was linked through a hidden ad on one of the sites that Nozomi probably runs."

"So my sister's playing a dumb prank."

"Speaking of pranks, having a page you have to do a bunch of stuff to unlock that contains 'information about the Headless Rider' is too far, in my opinion."

Kuon said nothing. Eventually, he gave up and exhaled. "Fine, fine. But that wasn't set up in a way that you could just click on it to get to the right page."

"I happen to have a bit of talent for puzzles and treasure hunts."

"This is what Sis gets for talking too much...," Kuon grumbled. Then he flipped a switch and continued, "Well, whatever. I was gonna tell you two about this at some point."

"..."

"Tell us what?" Yahiro was more confused than Himeka, who was simply skeptical.

Kuon gave his classmates a wicked grin and murmured, "My plan to make money."

"Make money?" Yahiro repeated. Now he, too, looked at Kuon skeptically.

The other boy's mouth curved upward, accentuating his expression. "Yeah. I created a *club* that solves problems in Ikebukuro and could earn us some good cash."

"And the name of the group is Snake Hands...your street alias, Yahiro."

♂♀

Shinra's apartment—near Kawagoe Highway

"Snake Hands, Snake Hands... Snake...Hands...!"

The words were chanted like some kind of curse in the spacious apartment.

"Ugh! Man! What's with this Snake Hands thing?! The more is *not* the merrier! Don't they know the saying 'The dose makes the poison'? Like, this is *literally* a case for 'moderation in all things'! Exactly! Precisely! Literally!"

Celty made an exasperated shrugging gesture and watched Shinra ranting and pouting like a child throwing a tantrum.

"What's the matter? Are you talking about Yahiro again?"

"That's right, Celty! You figured it out! Incredible, Celty—we are truly of one mind and spirit! Our hearts are connected! What's yours is yours, and what's mine is yours, except for one thing: Your *heart* is mine!"

It took merely seconds for Shinra's anger to do an about-face into a simpering smile. He grabbed Celty's hand. She easily brushed him aside and glanced at the laptop he had open.

It was displaying a message board thread discussing the Snake Hands rumors.

"I hear the Headless Rider's partner that people were talking about is known by the name Snake Hands."
"Yeah? Says who?"
"You know, that motorcycle gang... Dragon Zombies."

"*They're probably making stuff up.*"

"*But there's no other nickname we have for 'em. You can't keep saying the Headless Rider's partner.*"

"*Speaking of which, is the rider a guy or a girl?*"

"*People say they're a girl...which would make Snake Hands her boyfriend, I suppose.*"

"It's terrible! It's character assassination! *I'm* Celty's boyfriend! And the rumors aren't dying down; they're spreading further! Guess I've got no choice but to log on to the Internet encyclopedia and add something to the Headless Rider page. 'Celty lives with her boyfriend, Shinra Kishitani. The two lead a hot, steamy life together'..."

"*Citation needed!*"

"Ouch! Ouch!" Shinra yelped; he covered his head and rolled on the ground to defend himself against attack by a squeaky hammer made of shadow.

Celty rushed over to him, seemingly alarmed. "*Huh?! Whoops, I guess that was harder than I meant to make it... Sorry, are you all right?*"

"I'm all right, Celty. I love everything you give me, even pain!" Shinra said, perfectly recovered. He grabbed the shadow hammer. "Besides, I'm jealous of this Yahiro boy. He gets a hand-sewn outfit from you."

"*Is* hand sewn...*the right word for it?*"

"Um, Celty."

"*I'm not making one for you,*" she said promptly, not waiting for him to ask.

"Why not?!"

"*In your case, the first time I give in and allow you to have something, it leads to you asking me for everything.*"

"Hmm...can't deny that," Shinra admitted sadly.

Celty sighed and said, "*Listen, how about...we just wait until your next birthday?*"

She felt a bit embarrassed typing those words. Shinra's mouth briefly hung open with shock.

Then he exploded into joy. "Yesss! Thank you, Celty! Celty, thank you! I knew that day would come...and that knowledge alone is enough to keep me living on!"

"*You make such a big deal out of everything.*"

"My birthday is April second, so I've only got a bit more than eleven months to wait! Oh, boy!" Shinra raved, opening the calendar on his computer and typing in an event a year in the future. Celty felt relieved that his mood had recovered at least.

At that moment, Celty's cell phone—not the smartphone she used for conversation but the older flip phone for work—began to ring.

"Oh, you've got a new message, Celty... Huh?"

Shinra's body tensed again the moment he saw the name of the sender on the phone's external display.

SNAKE HANDS

The instant he saw those words, Shinra shouted, "Well, dammit! *Speak of the devil*—that's the phrase for this! I can't believe you even registered his contact information under that name! If you love point-less limbs on a snake so much, I'm going to have to inject myself with centipede DNA and *mrbl-grhggh*—"

"It's not what you're thinking," Celty typed, covering Shinra's mouth with shadow. She picked up the cell phone with one hand and typed dexterously on the smartphone with the other. *"This Snake Hands isn't Yahiro."*

"Huh?"

She pressed the confirmation button on the flip phone to accept the message as she conversed with Shinra.

"I told you, I've got a new side job.

"Shinra, Snake Hands is the name of the client giving me the job."

♂♀

The next day, Ikebukuro—private room of Pasela Karaoke

"Okay, so you're Yahiro!"

"Awww, he's so cute."

It was the first day of Golden Week in Ikebukuro.

Yahiro walked into the room Kuon instructed him to visit and saw an unfamiliar man and woman inside.

The man was narrow eyed and of mixed ethnicity while the woman had black hair and equally black fashion choices. The two of them seemed to be in their early twenties. They were seated in front of Kuon and spoke to him in a friendly manner from the moment he walked into the room.

"Hiya, I'm Walker Yumasaki."

"And I'm Erika Karisawa. Nice to meet you."

"Uh, hello…I'm Yahiro Mizuchi," he said, bowing politely, and sat down next to Kuon. "Um…do you know Kuon, then?"

"Not really," Kuon answered. "They're more friends of Aoba's, I guess. I've only had a few conversations with them on the street around town…"

"And how *is* Aobacchi?" the woman named Karisawa asked.

"Uh, the usual."

"Ah, cool. He was behaving himself recently after he caught Dotachin's ire." She cackled.

"Dotachin?" Yahiro asked, unsure of what that meant.

"Oh, just a personal joke. So what's up with you and Kuocchi…er, you and Kuon?" Yumasaki asked.

"We're friends," Yahiro said.

"Best friends?" Karisawa asked.

"I don't know. He's my first friend ever, so I wouldn't know the difference," he admitted without shame. Kuon just rolled his eyes.

"Oooh, ahhh, hohhh," Karisawa murmured, watching their reactions with great interest. "Your first friend ever. That's very nice, very sweet. Big Sis loves that scenario. And the way you seem embarrassed about it is very cute, Kuocchi."

"Scenario?" Yahiro repeated, even more confused.

Yumasaki nervously interjected, "Uh, you don't have to bother figuring out what she means most of the time."

"Oh, sorry, sorry. Big Sis turned you boys 2D in her head."

"2D…?" Yahiro mumbled.

"I'm serious, just ignore her," Yumasaki insisted.

It was at this point that the man named Yumasaki got to the matter that brought them together.

"Anyway, the truth is, we found the Snake Hands site and tried to make contact, and to our surprise, Kuon here was one of their members."

"I'll admit, I was startled when I saw your name in the mail in-box," Kuon said, shrugging.

Yahiro was wondering if this was another plot of some kind, but Kuon's expression didn't betray any of his usual bad acting, so Yahiro decided to take him at his word this time.

"So the thing about their request is," Kuon continued, "it's a job that I could have handled alone or through an acquaintance normally, but this time it's going to be trouble. I need more help."

"Why ask me? Aren't you usually hanging around with Aoba and his gang anyway?"

"It's not just anyone that I need for this. I need someone with a particular set of skills," Kuon said. He paused, then stared Yahiro right in the eyes. "Someone who is especially good at…fighting."

There was a brief silence.

"Oh…*mmbph!*"

"Down, Karisawa. Down. Down."

Yumasaki had clamped his hand over Karisawa's mouth, just before she could say something to the two younger boys.

Silence filled the room.

Yahiro stared at Kuon with empty eyes, then exhaled and replied, "Sorry, Kuon. I'm not inclined to do *that sort of thing* as a job…"

His apology was not sardonic or irritated. He sounded genuinely sorry that he couldn't help.

For his part, Kuon waved his hands and blurted out, "Wh-whoa, hold on! No, no, it's not that! I'm not asking you to be a hit man or some kind of bruiser!"

"You're not?" asked Yahiro.

"That's right," Yumasaki said. "Do we look like the kind of scumbags who would hire high schoolers to do a job like that?"

"…No."

"Right?" Kuon said, holding up his palms.

Yahiro bowed to his friend. "Okay. Sorry, Kuon. I had the wrong idea."

"…Uh, well…if you start apologizing *too* hard, it's going to make the rest of this request a lot harder…"

"?"

"It's not a job where you're gonna go around beating people up…but depending on events, there's a possibility *you* might get beat up…," Kuon said cryptically.

Karisawa clarified. "By the street attacker."

"Huh?"

"We're looking for the person attacking people on the street. We'd preferably like to find them before the police do, but we don't have much help in that regard. So we found the ad on that Ikebukuro website called *IkeNew!*—you know it? And there was some fiddling to do, but we managed to get your contact info."

"We just didn't think it would be someone we knew," Yumasaki added.

Karisawa nodded and looked at Yahiro. "But this is the street attacker we're talking about. And we can't put a child in danger, even if that child happens to be Kuocchi. But then he very confidently said, 'Yahiro would be all right, though!'"

"And that's when Kuocchi told us all about how this kid who got caught on video fighting Shizu-Shizu? The one everyone's been talking about? That it was *you*."

"…"

"So we figured, *Hey, maybe he's a better choice than some random adult who doesn't know what they're doing.* On the other hand, we're still against getting kids involved, and Dotachin would be mad, we figured. That's when Kuocchi pulled out the ace up his sleeve."

"Ace up his sleeve?" Yahiro repeated.

Yumasaki laughed and said, "When we heard Celty was part of your group, that set us totally at ease."

"Celty?" Yahiro looked over to Kuon.

Kuon just smirked and said, "Well, pretty much," and looked away to avoid eye contact.

"So, um…you two know Celty, then?" Yahiro asked.

"We go over to Celcchi's house now and then to hang out."

"Go over to her house…? Well, that makes it sound like *you're* best friends!"

"Why do I get the feeling that your definition of *best friends* has a very low bar to clear?!" Karisawa exclaimed. But she also put on a mysterious smile and muttered to herself, "That's pretty hot, too, though."

Yumasaki sighed and continued, "Anyway, we could have asked Celty right from the start, but it *is* a dangerous job."

"It's not something you can ask freely without guilt, like 'take a video of them' or something. Plus, I get the feeling that Celcchi would do it for free if I asked...and we didn't want that to happen. But if we can ask her in the form of a job, that might work."

"Yes. Which is why we're not asking you to take down the attacker. We just want you to help us gather stories from around town, to help get Celty closer to the right track. And at this point, we're too old to have personal connections inside of high school networks anymore."

"That makes sense," Yahiro said.

Kuon sensed that this was his chance for persuasion. "See, it's basically the same thing you did with the kidnappers earlier. It's just that there's a possibility the street attacker could spot you and go after you next, which is why you'd be perfect, since you're such a good fighter."

"No, I'm not..."

"Don't be modest! Whatever you happen to think about yourself, the moment you held your own against Shizuo, *everyone else* came to the agreement that you're a hell of a tough fighter! *You* gotta accept it, man! Plus, you don't want this hooligan running around town committing violence without end, do you? What if me or Himeka get attacked at some point?"

"That's true," Yahiro said, as simple as that. It was so easy, in fact, that it worried Kuon.

"Uh...listen, I know I shouldn't say this, since I'm the one who worked you up into saying yes, but are you *sure* you understand what I'm suggesting here?"

"Yeah. I've made up my mind now. I think violence is the only thing I'm good for. So at the very least, I want to make sure I don't use my talent the wrong way," Yahiro said without shame or hesitation. "At this point, the only thing that I know is right is protecting my friends, like Himeka and you. So I can help you with this if it means catching the attacker."

"You never know—it could be jumping out of the frying pan and into the fire. What if targeting this freak causes them to attack me or her next? Wouldn't that be putting the cart before the horse?" Kuon asked, rebuking Yahiro for not thinking it through.

But he wasn't ready for Yahiro's counterattack. "If I said the same thing and refused the job, you'd still try to handle it and simply not tell me, wouldn't you?"

"……"

Yahiro continued, "If you're going to make an enemy out of the attacker one way or the other, I'd rather face it head-on than stay ignorant and get caught unawares… It's less *scary* that way."

Kuon thought that was rather strange, and he couldn't find anything to say in return.

Yahiro turned to the other two and bowed his head. "I'd like to help, if you're all right with that."

Karisawa smiled. "You don't have to be so stuffy about it. We'll pay you, too. This is a business deal, you see. You can discuss the details about that with Kuon. Ultimately, we're paying you for information collection, so if you think it's getting dangerous, disengage at once, okay? You might be tough, but leave the dangerous stuff to the adults. Don't be stubborn about that, all right?"

"Thank you," Yahiro said, bowing yet again. Then a question crossed his mind. "But why are you two hunting for the attacker? Why not have the police handle it?" He wondered if maybe their relatives or friends had been among the victims thus far.

But by way of an answer, Yumasaki pulled a stack of books out of his backpack and began to line them up on the table.

Yahiro tilted his head. He realized he was staring at volumes of a manga series. Even he recognized the title: *Owl of the Peeping Dead*. However, it was more famous for its anime and live-action movie.

"The most mainstream one is the anime, but lending you all the DVDs at once is too much, so we figured the manga would be the easiest way for you to get into it," Yumasaki said, grinning. He offered the books to Kuon and Yahiro. "Before we can properly discuss this incident, we need you to research—with these!"

Kuon stared in skepticism. Even he hadn't been aware of the finer details of the situation. "Really? I mean, I know the attacker's supposed to be cosplaying a character from this, but…"

"If they're dressing up to commit a crime, they're not cosplaying! That's an insult to the original story!" Yumasaki fumed abruptly. He grabbed the mic from the desk, turned it on, then bellowed into it so that his words filled the room.

"It's not *OPD*'s fault! *OPD*'s just fine!"

*   *   *

Ten minutes later

"But then, in the middle of the story, something unbelievable comes to light... We find out there's a zombie who lost its conscious mind—*and then regains it.* And that's completely shocking to our protagonist, the Owl. He thinks, *All these zombies I've been killing?* assuming they were forever gone. Maybe there's a way to *save* them. Maybe the Zombie Protection Group was right, and they're just sick and need to be cured..."

"Um, thank you, Mr. Yumasaki, that was a really great description, but we'll read the manga, we promise. You can stop there...," Kuon insisted.

"Aaaah! What have I done?! I'm so sorry! You were going to read the manga, and I just spoiled the whole thing for you...! I'm a failure of an otaku! I'll carry this shame for life!" Yumasaki wailed.

Yahiro tried to reassure him. "It's all right. I already know how the story goes."

"Huh? Have you seen or read the series, Yahiro?"

"No, I saw the live-action movie."

"Oh, the movie! That was done pretty well, too, I have to say! The whole project started as a fake zombie info site online before becoming an anime and manga, and then came the live-action! But from what I hear, the movie was in production before the anime, so it's possible they envisioned the whole project based around the live-action first."

Karisawa's eyes sparkled as she joined in. "Yeah, I wasn't sure if it would work as live-action, but they really got into it!"

"I agree. It was low budget and didn't have much CG, but that just made Tenjin Zakuroya's zombie effects that much more effective," Yahiro said.

"Wow, Yahiro! You know who Tenjin Zakuroya is? That's impressive!"

At last, the conversation was reaching the typical excitement found in a karaoke room. Kuon, feeling abruptly left behind, addressed Yahiro. "H-hey, you know about this *Owl of the Something*?"

"I don't know about the manga or anime...but I watched the movie back at home."

"You watch movies?"

"Uh, yeah?" Yahiro said, feeling slightly insulted by the question.

"I didn't have any friends then, so about the only thing I would do at home was watch movies on my own."

"That's too sad. You're making me feel bad for asking."

"Really? *You* feel bad?"

"Look, if you were one of those lonely people desperate for attention and said that in order to be, like, 'Look at me—don't you feel sorry for me?' I'd just be, like, 'Yeah, yeah, sure,' and ignore you. But you talk like it was normal for you, like it's an objective fact. I have no idea how to react to that! And I feel bad about being honest and saying I feel sorry for you!"

This sudden outburst took Yahiro by surprise. "You feel sorry for me?" he asked, looking around uncertainly.

Karisawa leaned forward and rubbed Yahiro's head. "You're fine, you're fine. We feel sorry for you, but it's cute. In a cute way."

"?!" He tensed up at the sudden touch of his head, like a cat whose tail had been grabbed.

To keep the mood from getting any weirder, Yumasaki stepped in and said, "Anyway, that's the thing! That's the thing! I hate this attacker! An old fellow independent artist friend of mine is one of the people in WWW, and I know these attacks have really been hurting them!"

"Ah, I see."

If one of his friends was suffering as a result, that certainly would go a long way to explaining Yumasaki's rage, Yahiro decided. But he did have a question. "Um…if Celty does catch the culprit, what's going to happen to them after that?"

Yumasaki and Karisawa replied to this very natural question by sharing a look, then beaming.

"We just want to talk to whoever's doing it."

"Yes, very politely," Erika noted.

"And we want to ask why they would do something that harms the reputation of anime and its fans… That's all. It's really that simple."

"Exactly, we just want to talk. Nice and slowly. Physically speaking."

Yahiro's cowardly instincts sensed a terrible, horrible pressure behind their smiles. He decided that it was not worth asking them for more details.

♂♀

One hour later—the hallway of the karaoke establishment

Once they were done talking business, Karisawa and Yumasaki began what they called a Get-to-Know-You Gala, which was actually an anime theme song marathon.

Yahiro hardly recognized a single one of them, but he was happy that they responded well to the movie theme he requested, and he came away from his first karaoke experience feeling fairly satisfied.

It had been nerve-racking, singing a song he liked in front of other people for the first time—but when he left to look for the bathroom, he ran into Kuon in the hallway, who was on a call.

"...Yeah. Anyway, I'll call you later, Sis." He hung up, then shrugged at Yahiro. Then he put on a cocky smile and said snottily, "You angry?"

"About what?"

"Huh...? About *me*."

"?" Yahiro was honestly confused. Had Kuon done something meant to make him angry?

Maybe there was something that people in Tokyo would've been angry about. In that case, it was important that he figure out what it was so he didn't accidentally do it to someone else.

When Kuon noticed him thinking hard, he snapped, "I did tons of stuff you should be mad about. Why don't you get that?"

"Get what?"

"...Don't you get that I'm using you?" Kuon said, then clicked his tongue at himself for being so direct. He started ripping into Yahiro instead. "I told those two that you were the guy fighting Shizuo Heiwajima on video. I told them you were a good fighter and involved you in something dangerous. I'm using you as bait for my own gain. Don't you get that? Besides, you must've heard from my sister that I only approached you from the start because I wanted to use you!"

"Yeah."

"Yeah...? That's it...?"

"But is that really something to be mad about?"

Kuon was unable to think of anything to say to that. The only sound in the hallway was faint singing coming from the soundproofed private rooms.

With furrowed brows, Kuon eventually asked, "So...when *do* you get mad?"

It had been such a shockingly in-character answer from Yahiro that Kuon's irritation simply vanished, replaced by pure bewilderment.

As Yahiro thought that over, his expression darkened. "Hmm... Well, there was the time someone tried to run me over with a dump truck and then got mad when they failed, so they tried to burn down my house... Also, I'm mad when people go after my mom and dad instead of me... I got really mad those times."

"...Uh, yeah, when you bring out crazy examples like that, it doesn't exactly help answer my question." Kuon sighed heavily. "Listen, don't you worry about me doing the same things those people did? Don't you ever imagine me doing something crazy like using not just you but your family *and* Himeka, dragging them into something really dangerous?"

"That would suck."

"Then you get mad *before* things get that serious! You can tell the difference between good and bad, right? It should be obvious to you that I'm a bad guy!"

But despite Kuon's insistence that he should be labeled an evildoer, Yahiro's response was blunt. "Kuon, I happen to think that people's natures can't be labeled so simply as 'good' or 'bad.' At the very least, a person's nature isn't something so easily understood."

"......"

"I get blatantly evil people, like serial killers or those people attacking others on the street. But I don't think I could label you and Himeka as good or bad for anything short of those extreme examples. The thing is, I know that the stuff I've done is just as awful as the stuff the attacker's doing. So I can't point the finger and describe others that way. I don't have the right."

He sounded sad and clenched his fists. Yahiro told his friend, "So if you think you're evil, and you want me to stop you by force..."

He paused.

Yahiro considered his own case and repeated what he knew as it passed through his mind.

"I don't think I would pick up on that, so I'd want you to tell me. I don't think I could make that decision on my own. Instead, I *can* keep myself ready to hit you at any moment."

It was as honest and plain as he could possibly be.

"That's a crazy request to put on someone's shoulders," Kuon said.

"Sorry."

"Why do you just...*trust* people like that? Especially after you've thought so hard about it." Kuon clenched his jaw. Frustration entered his voice again. "I hate that about you."

"Sorry. I'll try to work on that."

"Don't gimme that. Besides, I'm not saying you're wrong." Kuon clicked his tongue again. He started walking away, done with the conversation. As he passed, Yahiro gave him a faint smile.

"You're right... Thanks for worrying about me."

"...!"

Kuon spun back, grimacing, but Yahiro was already on his way as well, rounding the corner to the bathroom. Kuon put a hand on the wall and clicked his tongue yet again, quite loud this time.

"Dammit. He really throws me off my game..."

Envisioning the face of the man he both hated and aspired to be, he scowled.

"If he were a real scumbag like Izaya Orihara, I could use him and abuse him guilt-free..."

♂♀

Ikebukuro—night

"Well, Mr. Horada, so long!"

"A'ight."

The man split off from his younger companions and headed home alone.

Horada was once a principal member of the Blue Squares and had even taken over the Yellow Scarves earlier. He was a hallowed figure in the history of street gangs—or so he liked to tell himself.

In truth, he was merely a small-time thug who happened to ride the waves at the right time and place, but his exploits were indeed legends of a sort, and his name was fairly well-known among people in his part of society.

However, Horada understood that color-repping street gangs were disappearing from Tokyo.

A number of them had reverted to an older form of delinquency, the classic *bosozoku* motorcycle gang, while others shifted into a different kind of mob, the *gurentai* young ruffians.

Horada had been in prison meanwhile, left behind by the changing of the times. Now he was left to scheme about how his glory days might once again return.

There were former followers who still admired him, but he had many old enemies who hated his guts.

In order to climb to the top in Ikebukuro, he needed absolute power. With that in mind, he recalled one such strength that seemed within reach.

Man, ever since then, I haven't found the right moment to get an in with that Yahiro Mizuchi guy. I really gotta let him know I was the one who found the kidnappers' hideout and make him feel grateful to me...

During the recent case of mass kidnappings, which turned out to be false, Horada managed to find the hideout of those who abducted Himeka Tatsugami, albeit almost entirely by coincidence.

After making its way to the younger guys in the Blue Squares, the information had somehow made it to Yahiro Mizuchi himself, and the whole incident had resolved itself safely.

That meant he'd earned himself a favor, but if he tried to call that in too eagerly, he might get that debt repaid in a single act. He'd never manage to lure the guy into his stable of perpetual companions.

I shouldn't force the issue. I just gotta imprint on his mind that I'm the guy who helped him... But on the other hand, I dunno if spreading the story around is smart, either... Kinda seemed like there were Awakusu-kai and Dragon Zombie guys at the scene, too. Don't need them coming after me in revenge...

He allowed himself a little shiver and turned his attention to a vending machine at the end of the alley.

Hey, I'm feelin' a bit thirsty. Could go for a coffee.

He stopped in front of the machine and bought himself a can of unsweetened coffee with creamer. The can clunked as it fell down into the pickup port.

It was just an ordinary vending machine. Horada reached for the opening, just like he always would.

But then he noticed something was wrong.

"...Huh?"

It was like a shadow in the corner of his vision had moved. He turned his head to the left.

Someone was standing there, wearing a suit of black pajamas.

"Whaaa—?!" he yelped involuntarily, startled by the stranger suddenly right next to the vending machine with him. But his alarm turned to irritation as he realized it was just regular clothes in a *kigurumi* onesie style. "What the hell's your problem? Dressed like a freak! Fuck off—I'll kill you!"

It wasn't the most creative threat, but harassing people and grabbing their shirts was something Horada was used to doing—except that this time, he stopped when he saw the figure lift a narrow object wrapped in a white cloth.

He recognized it immediately. Based on the shape, it was a hammer wrapped in bandages. As he came to that realization, the bandaged hammer swung downward violently.

"Whuaaah?!" he screamed, toppling sideways and just barely evading the blow. "Wh-wha...what the fuck?! Do you know who I am?! Which gang are you with?! Huh?!"

Horada had no interest in the news, whether on TV or on paper, so it never occurred to him that this might actually be the street attacker.

"Some weird-ass clothes you've got..."

But even he could clearly see that the person facing him meant him harm. He jumped to his feet as the person clad in the black onesie swung the hammer.

"Don't mess with me!" He hurled the unopened can of coffee at the enemy.

"—!"

The person in the onesie pajamas blocked the can by holding both hands over their stomach. That was enough time for Horada to close the gap.

Quicker than they could lift the hammer again, Horada punched the hooded head as hard as he could.

The mysterious attacker flew backward and toppled to the ground in front of the vending machine.

"Moron... You thought some little freak like you could take out *the* Horada?! Huh?!" Horada roared, approaching with the intent to kick his attacker in the face and finish them off for good.

"Guh?!"

Something struck him, and the upper half of his vision went dark.
He stumbled and turned to see another figure wearing the same *kigurumi* pajamas...
"Gangin' up...on a guy... Cowardly...piesh...a...shit..."

Just before he lost consciousness, slurring his words, Horada saw a bandage-wrapped hammer hurtling down at him.
Part of the white fabric was dyed red with his own blood.

♂♀

The next morning

"There has been an update in the ongoing series of street attacks: a new victim.

"The latest to fall prey to the attacker is a twenty-two-year-old unemployed resident of Tokyo by the name of..."

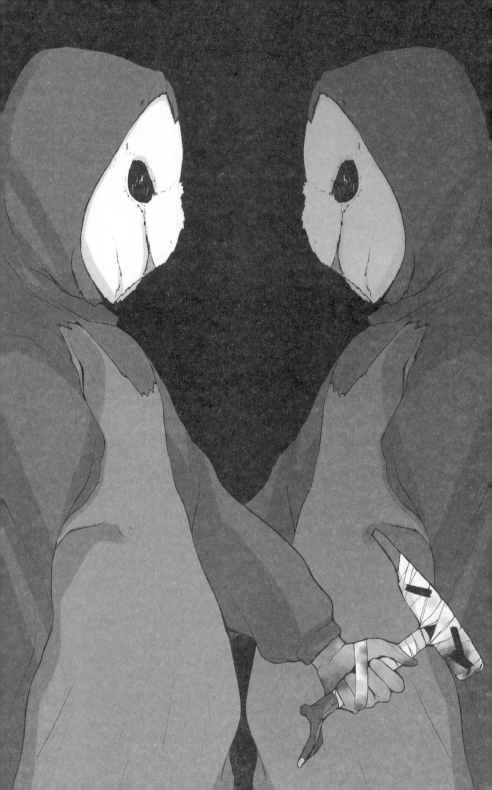

INTERMISSION
Online Rumors

On the Ikebukuro information site IkeNew! Version I.KEBU.KUR.O

```
New Post: [Warfare Breaks Out!] Former gang
member hit by street attacker [Return of the
Yellow Scarves?]
```

"Where did the Headless Rider go?" (Rehosted from *Tokyo Warrior* online site)

In the early hours of the morning, an anonymous call placed from a public phone claimed that a man had been beaten on the street. Police arrived at the scene and discovered a man with a wounded head.

The person who called in the tip had left the scene, perhaps fearing retaliation. The man was transported to a hospital, where his injuries were labeled not life-threatening.

According to the tip, the attacker wore black clothes in the style of a onesie costume and struck the victim with what looked like a white stick. Police are investigating whether the attack is related to the string of recent incidents.

The man was identified as a prominent member of a former color-based street gang from Ikebukuro, apparently leading some to suggest that it was actually the work of another gang of some kind, mocked up to look like the street attacker. Various groups are on heightened alert for the possibility of a new wave of gang violence.

—*(The rest of this article can be read at the original link)*

For reference: a comment from Shinichi Tsukumoya on another news site

Whether or not it has anything to do with the street attacks, it's true that the leader of Dragon Zombies returning to town has shifted the power balance with other groups like the younger *gurentai*. There's a new name being thrown about, Snake Hands—though I don't know if that's a person's nickname or a group moniker.

I'm curious to see if he, she, or they become the next eye of the storm in Ikebukuro.

The victim in this case was a fellow who attracted much attention in the heyday of the Dollars, so that could light the embers from that past era or is a sign they're already lit. We ought to be wary.

Comment from IkeNew! *Administrator*

According to the online rumors, they say it was Mr. H, who just got out of pwison.

Some say he was the leader of the Yellow Scarves, if onwy fow a moment.

A scawwy man out of jaiw...

A free man no longer being punished by the law, perhaps struck down by his victims out of revenge—or maybe he only looks tough due to his reputation and was easily taken down by the cuwpwit?

If it's a stweet waw, who's the attackew?

Dragon Zombies?

Jan-Jaka-Jan?

Dollars?

Yellow Scarves?

Blue Squares?

Toramaru from Saitama?

Or is there some new power in Ikebukuro we've never heard of?

It's scawwy! It's fweaky!

The stweet attackew's scawwy, but so are the thugs forming up new gangs.

God save us aww.

Admin: Rira Tailtooth Zaiya

A selection of representative twits from the social network Twittia

Have you noticed how Tsukumoya changes his writing style by the site or book?

→When he's being serious, he writes normally, but his style gets pretty wild when he's being blunt.

→I wonder which is his true voice?

→It's like there are several of him.

→Maybe there are.

So it was Horada who got knocked out?

→Sounds like it.

→lmao. Suck it.

→That's kinda mean.

→He deserves every awful thing that happens to him.

→Yeah. He was just Izumii's dingleberry, but he acts like he's such hot shit.

→I heard he used to have a gun, though.

→That's crazy. Hope they execute him soon.

*   *   *

So is this really the street attacker? Or is it just another person with beef?

→ Has to be the attacker. There are witnesses. Would gangs with beef do cosplay?

  → The tip was anonymous, right? Could've been a gang enemy calling it in.

  → For example, say you knock him out and report the attack. You gotta give visual details, right?

  → Then the police will believe it was the street attacker, right?

  → And they won't suspect your dopey little gang, right?

  → Wow, like, this is a big brain moment, right?

    → Uh, you realize that pretty much anyone could have come up with that?

      → Why don't you shut up, right?

    → Wow, you're sooo smart /s

      → You think that's funny? I'm seconds away from blocking you.

  → I think that's possible. In fact, all the attacks could be by a motorcycle gang.

    → It seems likely. Maybe not all the older attacks, though.

      → What makes them any different?

        → Why would a motorcycle gang do cosplay to attack couples and grandpas on the street?

It was the Headless Rider.

  → You can't just blame everything on the Rider!

    → Well, that whole faked group kidnapping was indirectly their fault.

      → It's not right to blame every little thing on the Headless Rider.

→The Headless Rider is a very sweet person.

→Those people who faked the kidnapping did that on their own. They're more like antis than true believers.

→In fact, some people say it was the Rider who solved that kidnapping.

→You're so desperate.

→I looked at his profile and it says he's a "black market doctor" loooool

→B L A C K M A R K E T D O C T O R
i'm dead

I wonder what happened with Snake Hands.

→Haven't heard of anything since.

→That was the Headless Rider's girlfriend, right?

→Not boyfriend?

→Is the Headless Rider a girl?

→I've heard as much.

→She totally is. I've seen her get off her bike, and her figure is definitely feminine.

→You just have to look from the side, and you'll see she's got a chest.

→So that would mean, assuming she's not gay, Snake Hands must be her boyfriend.

→Wrong.

→Snake Hands is NOT her boyfriend.

→Now that's a relationship that's truly as irrelevant as hands on a snake.

→Shut up, "black market doctor." She's not gonna give you a medical license lol

* (DMs between two accounts)

*   *   *

Hey, Shinra. I'm out on a job, so I'll tell you this from here: Knock it off.

You sound like a troll.

You're usually so calm and collected. Why do you freak out about Yahiro like this?

→Sorry, Celty. I'm ashamed of myself.

→This Yahiro gets to fight at your side, but I can't do that.

→I'm so jealous that you get to watch each other's backs!

→Uh...you realize that's not what's going on between us, right?

→I swear. You never got this jealous when I would talk with Shizuo or Izaya.

→Yeah... I know I'm being weird.

→Ever since two years ago, I've had something on my mind.

→Remember when you were so worried for me when I got kidnapped by another woman?

→I think, now that another man is coming on to you, a part of me feels like I should be acting jealous...

→I appreciate the sentiment, but you're going about it all wrong.

→Yahiro is not "coming on to me," for one thing.

→Anyway, I get it. We can talk about this more when I get home.

Also, Shinra? You should delete that "black market doctor" thing in your profile.

→ It's fine—nobody believes it. I won't get turned in to the authorities.

→ Er, that's not what I mean...

→ It's just really embarrassing to see everyone make fun of you for it...

CHAPTER
2

CHAPTER 2
Let's Live on the Straight and Narrow

Something is wrong.
  Why did this happen?
  I eliminated the scum.
  I did something good.

  Why is the Dark Owl still the villain?
  Why are all the scum treated as the victims?

♂♀

Early evening—Raira General Hospital, private room

Horada woke up to the pain of everything in his body creaking.

Several days had passed since he was brought to the hospital after the attack. He'd suffered a skull fracture, but miraculously there was no damage to the brain underneath. Worse actually were the numerous kicks he'd suffered after blacking out. He had broken ribs and his collarbone, and he recalled being told that recovery would take months.

"*Aaaugh...* That hurts... Shit. Are these painkillers even working?"

He knew the police would be by for questioning once they heard he was conscious again, but Horada was keeping them at bay by claiming he was still feeling groggy. That was actually true. In this state, he might actually follow their lead and say something he really didn't want to say to the cops.

The police hadn't left a guard for his room. They didn't seem to be worried about the attacker going after one specific person. If there had been one, Horada would have requested they leave anyway, claiming it would be a distraction.

But what do I tell the cops? If I say I got done in by two people and admit I fought back and hit one, that's bad for me, right? Gotta think of how to explain this so it's a hundred percent self-defense... Actually, it looks bad for me if I got knocked out by the street attacker, too. Maybe I should claim there were, like, ten of 'em...

He wasn't thinking about the possibilities of being caught in a lie through eyewitness testimony or charged with disrupting an investigation; Horada was solely occupied by the thought of his reputation.

"I swear, the next time I see those freaks, I'm gonna kill 'em... Owww!" He grumbled as his entire body creaked and cracked.

He was going to lie back down and think hard about what to do next—when he noticed something moving in the corner of his vision.

"Wh-who's there?"

Probably a nurse, he assumed, gingerly craning his painful neck.

What he saw instead was a man with very distinctive sunglasses and facial burns, sitting in the round guest chair in the corner of the room.

"What's this?" The man grinned and closed the magazine of adult photography he was perusing. He got to his feet. "I heard you were still in and out of it, so I figured this was a waste...but you seem full of pep to me."

"...!"

Horada's entire body shivered, regardless of the creaking, and his teeth chattered. "I...Iii...Izumii..."

Ran Izumii—the man who had led the Blue Squares when Horada was a member.

Izumii had been in prison for a while, but he got out around the time Horada went in. Word on the street was that he was currently a junior member of the Awakusu-kai.

"You've been through the wringer, man. I heard the story...and came to pay you a visit."

"Y-y-you did! Thank you!" Horada said, automatically adjusting his tone to come off as nonthreatening.

Just once, Izumii came to visit the prison where Horada had served his sentence. They did see each other—but Horada would have been happy never seeing the man again.

Izumii would freely do insane things like breaking the legs of an abducted girl with a hammer. Then a fellow member he betrayed hit him with a Molotov cocktail. Ever since his stint in the slammer, it was like he'd lost a few extra screws in addition to the ones he was already missing.

"U-uh, wow, Izumii, you've lost a lot of weight! I barely recognize you!" Horada blabbered, alarmed by the sudden turn of events and trying to get on Izumii's good side. Each word he spoke made his whole body hurt, but that was a minor issue compared to his fear of the other man. Painfully, he tried to put on a friendly smile.

"Oh, did I? If you want to slim down, I got a great suggestion," Izumii said, shrugging and pulling something out of his jacket. It was a small hammer made of hardened rubber. He continued, "If I break your jaw, you can't eat and gain any more weight, eh?"

"...!"

Izumii smacked the hammer into his palm playfully.

Horada's mind was trapped between two parallel terrors: Izumii himself and the weapon that put him in the hospital days ago. If that hammer had a cloth bandage wrapped around it, he might have screamed.

"Th-that's not funny, Izumii," he said, attempting a pleasant smile.

Izumii smirked back at him and changed the subject. "You know, this is the hospital where they took that chick whose legs I broke. You remember that? The girlfriend of that guy Kida from the Yellow Scarves. The one you nabbed."

"Huh? Oh yeah, right."

"Maybe she was even in this very room. I bet she left, like, a ghostly imprint here, a living curse. That would explain it if your legs suddenly turned up broken for no clear reason."

"......"

Fwap! Ba-dump!

Fwap! Ba-dump!

Horada's racing heart matched the rhythm of the hammer striking Izumii's palm.

Horada had no idea what Izumii intended to do—which was exactly what made it easy for him to imagine that hammer hurtling down onto him. Horada swallowed hard.

"So here's the thing," Izumii started.

"Y-yesh?!" Horada wheezed, the air shooting out of his lungs as Izumii leaned in.

"You know this can't end here, right?"

"H-heh?"

"See, this hammer is kinda my *thing*, ya know? All the other guys in my line of business are talkin' about how I went outta my way to punish you for bein' a fuckup. Normally, I wouldn't care what people say, but what if Mr. Aozaki or Mr. Akabayashi hear about it? I can't have that."

He clenched the hammer and pressed the tip hard against Horada's nose.

"Hrrng." Horada withstood the pain, feeling a cold sweat break out.

Izumii continued, "Of course, if a story gets around sayin' I needed to go to the trouble of puttin' on a costume and ambushing you in order to punish you, that looks bad for me, right? You get what I'm saying, Horada."

"Y-yesh!"

"You used to roam around the city with your boys, right? Use them; do whatever you gotta. Just find this damn street attacker before the cops do and bring them to me. Got that?"

"…!"

He knew it was an absurd order, but there was no way he could defy the other man. Despite the fog of his recent sleep, Horada's mind raced through how he might carry out the command.

Before the cops?! Does that mean I shouldn't mention that there were actually two of them? And how will I get the people… The people—oh!

An idea occurred to him. He hesitantly offered it to Izumii. "Uh, w-well, do…do you think I could use…the current Blue Squares?"

"Huh? Do it yourself," said Izumii, who seemed to be just now remembering that they existed, too.

Horada continued, "W-w-well, you know, y-your brother's with them, so I thought maybe I shouldn't let him get hur—ghrblhflgh?!"

The instant he mentioned Izumii's brother, the hammer pressed down harder.

"Why would I worry about that piece of shit Aoba? Huh? What, do I hafta worry about his calories and nutrients every time he eats a meal? I gotta cook him a balanced breakfast each morning, do I?"

"F-fhorry!" Horada apologized, despite the unfairness of Izumii's anger. All he could do was plead for forgiveness from the man's murderous rage.

"As long as you learn. You're a former big shot with the Blue Squares, and Aoba's a current member who came after you. That's all there is between you, right?" Izumii said, craning his neck so hard to look at Horada that it cracked. "If he breaks down, well—that's just what's gotta happen. Use him and abuse him."

It was as though Izumii hoped to see his own brother fall to pieces.

♂♀

The next day—a bowling alley in Ikebukuro

"So my question is, do you feel like helping look for the attacker?" Aoba Kuronuma asked.

Yahiro considered this, still holding the ball.

"What's wrong?" Aoba asked.

"Oh…just…thinking how coincidences *do* happen."

It was in the middle of Golden Week, the week of holidays. Aoba invited Yahiro out to bowl. When he got to the alley, he found Aoba and a number of nasty-looking companions.

They were all wearing their regular clothes, not school uniforms. Yahiro was wearing an outfit he'd just bought days earlier. At first, they were having fun doing regular bowling, but around the third game, Aoba brought up something while they bowled at the same lane.

He said that a former member of his group named Horada had been attacked on the street, and the man had ordered Aoba to search for the attacker to enact revenge.

According to Aoba, Horada was still in the hospital, but his injuries weren't life-threatening. Aoba had no idea that Yahiro was already searching for the attacker, albeit for a different reason.

"You know we're not *just* a group of friends, right…? After the last thing, especially," Aoba explained.

"Yes. A couple people have told me about the Blue Squares," Yahiro replied.

"Oh yeah? What did they say?"

"You don't have a good reputation."

Aoba burst into laughter. "There is such a thing as being too honest, Yahiro."

"I'm just scared that if I lie, someone will find out later," he replied seriously.

Aoba just giggled. "Yeah, not a good reputation. But an older guy from the group with an even *worse* reputation is someone I have to respect. Sticking up for him is sticking up for the gang," he explained. He didn't look anything like the honor student he played at school. "So the more people we have, the better. I was hoping you could help out."

"That's fine."

"...You replied awfully quick. I assumed you would say no."

"Why?"

"I reached out to Kuon, too, but he says he's busy with a new business venture. I just assumed you were doing that, too."

"Well, yes. I am."

"You admit it?!" Apparently, Aoba had been trying to trick him into saying it, but that wasn't necessary. "Don't you get that you should keep that sort of stuff a secret from me?"

"No, really?"

"Yes, really," Aoba said, lightly mocking him.

Since he had so much success eliciting information about Kuon just a moment earlier, Aoba followed up with another question. "So what kind of business is it?"

"Oh, that part is a secret."

"..."

"Sorry, it's nothing personal to you. We're not supposed to tell other people in general about what we do. If you really want to know, I would suggest asking Kuon yourself."

It was a frank dismissal of the question but not one made out of any malice toward Aoba. If anything, there was always some level of caution, but that was just Yahiro's cowardly nature. It was akin to a caution born of paranoia, like he was always wondering, *What if all*

*these people are under some kind of hypnosis and they suddenly pull
out metal bats and beat on me? How should I get away?*

That was normal for Yahiro, and Aoba understood that. That was
why Aoba decided that he wasn't going to get an answer under any circumstances. He got back to the topic at hand. "Well, that's fine. I'll ask
Kuon if there's any way I can get a piece of his business."

"Thank you."

"So about this street attacker... The truth is, you owe Mr. Horada a
debt, too, so you really ought to help avenge him."

"Uh...I do?"

"Yep. Remember that faked kidnapping?"

"Yeah."

"The person who helped us look for your friend, uh...Miss Tatsugami?
That was Mr. Horada."

"!"

Yahiro's eyes widened.

The thought had slipped to the wayside in the chaos, but he *did*
recall that Aoba knew where to find them and said he heard it from
someone else. If that person was this Horada guy, then it was true that
Yahiro did owe him a debt.

"Oh, I see... Well, then I really *do* have to help."

"Yep. So if we find the attacker, we wanna nab 'em first before we
hand them over to the cops."

"..."

Nab 'em. That choice of words put a thought into Yahiro's mind.

"Uh, not that we're talking about killing them or anything," Aoba
quickly added.

"Either way, holding someone against their will is a crime."

"True, I suppose. But if you wanna get technical, what you did at that
mansion was a crime, too. There's such a thing as excessive self-defense."

At that point, the bowling order had come around to Aoba.

"Oh, it's my turn to bowl," he said. While he went up there to roll,
Yahiro considered what he'd said.

*Hmm. What should I do? I definitely don't think we should beat up that
person. But it's true that giving back what you've been given is how I've always
done this kind of thing. I can't claim that it's completely unacceptable...*

The real question is, if I find the person and catch them, who do I take them to first? Karisawa's group or this Horada person? Karisawa and Yumasaki said they just wanted to talk...so maybe I could go to them first, then Horada, and if it starts to get out of hand, I'll stop them and go to the police.

It's just really important that we don't gang rush this person. I just don't have the right to stop them...

Aoba rolled a spare, earning him cheers and jeers from his friends on the adjacent lanes. He came back to the seats, and Yahiro stood up to take his turn.

As they passed, Yahiro said, "I really don't think you should look for vengeance."

"Oh yeah? Why not?" Aoba asked.

Yahiro went into his delivery rather than answer the question. He hurled the ball, then turned back to Aoba without watching the result.

In his mind, he envisioned the past—of his hands covered with blood and the broken bodies of his attackers, a sight that repeated itself many times back home.

"Giving back everything they give you...is pretty painful, you know?"

The monitor over their lane lit up, playing the sound that indicated a strike.

"Oh...I got a strike?"

He'd just tossed it off without a second thought and assumed it would be a gutterball. He stood at the ball return with mild surprise; he'd been expecting to take his second roll in just a moment.

Aoba patted the younger boy on the shoulder and beamed. "You don't need to tell *me* that."

It was a thin smile, a look that Yahiro never saw from him.

"But the thing is, Yahiro...I happen to *like* that kind of pain."

Ikebukuro West Gate Park—evening

"And that's the story. What do you think I should do?"

It was the hour when the sun hid behind the buildings. Yahiro sat on a metal tube bench, talking to Himeka.

"Well, if you're unsure enough that you'd come right to *me* for advice, I don't think there's anything I could tell you...," she said with exasperation, though her expression was the same as ever.

After his time with Aoba and his friends, Yahiro called up Himeka to consult with her. She just happened to be near Ikebukuro Station, so they met up at the park.

Himeka was technically another member of Snake Hands, so Yahiro did not hesitate to tell her about the job request to help find the recent attacker.

To his surprise, however, Himeka already knew about that. According to her, she told Kuon that if it was something she could help with, she would. A few days later, Nozomi gave her a call about it. That was when she heard all about the attacks.

"...So you accepted the job, too?"

"Yes, I suppose so."

"Chasing down this attacker seems like a pretty dangerous thing to do...," Yahiro said, which was perfectly accurate.

Himeka replied, "I'm surprised to hear you say that, given that you went searching for the Headless Rider when she was rumored to be kidnapping people."

"That's a good point."

She exhaled. "Well, I'm not intending to get into any danger. But I feel like not doing anything is going to end up with Kuon and Nozomi doing something reckless, so I can't sit by and do nothing..."

"Yeah, that's a good point," Yahiro said, realizing that Himeka was thinking along the same lines as he was. "In any case, it can only be a good thing if the street attacks stop. But I've got two groups of people asking to see the attacker before we hand them over to the police. If I happen to stumble across the attacker knocked out on the street and I'm lucky enough to capture them right there, which one do you think I should take them to first?"

"That's a difficult question. Can I say something first?"

"What?"

"What do you mean by if they're 'knocked out on the street'?" she asked.

"Let's say," Yahiro replied, "they tried to attack Shizuo Heiwajima, and he knocked them out..."

"...Well, that would certainly be a good reason for them to be knocked out," Himeka said without expression. She twisted at the waist, staring Yahiro right in the face. "Couldn't *you* beat the attacker if you ran into them?"

"I'm too scared to fight the street attacker."

"I can't believe I'm hearing that from someone who was beating up motorcycle gangs and mobsters..."

"I was really scared then, too. But I was more afraid of *not* doing anything then. That's all it was," Yahiro said, a note of unease in his eyes. "I've been fighting all the time, so I'm not so good with human relationships and mind games and all that stuff... I don't know what the right answer is."

"It's all right if you're wrong. In fact, you'll learn faster that way."

"I'm scared."

"I'm telling you, it's really strange to hear you say the word *scared*, each and every time," Himeka said, as expressionless as ever. "You had a reason for using your strength the way you did. So why does the street attacker do what they're doing?"

"That's a good question." Yahiro had completely overlooked the matter of the attacker's motive. In his mind, the street attacker was like a psychotic murderer from a movie—or a part of the stage backdrop that would attack without reason.

However—as much as he didn't like to think of it, because it sounded like an excuse—he himself was called a monster, and *he* certainly had his reasons for using violence.

Yahiro didn't want to imagine people walking around town, deciding to kill others for no less arbitrary a reason than that the sky was blue. But he was just as afraid of casting aside the possibility that the attacker was simply born to commit violence. He had to keep both reasons in mind.

"So...why do they attack people? Why hit them?" Yahiro wondered aloud. "I've been struck from behind by a hammer many times before...and usually those people were saying, 'I'll kill you.' What were they planning to do once they'd killed me...?"

By this point, Himeka was used to Yahiro talking about extremely disturbing experiences. She suggested, "As an amateur, the first thing I think is maybe they have some kind of weird sexual thing where hitting and hurting people makes them feel good. Or they're under some kind of delusion that if they don't attack people, they'll die… Or maybe they're *not* actually attacking people randomly."

"It's not random?"

"I'm saying maybe the victims have something in common. It might look like they're indiscriminate attacks, but perhaps they're choosing their victims based on clear criteria that only the attacker understands. In that case, the motive would be very important."

"Something in common… I never thought of that."

Yahiro had heard the outline of the incident on the radio and such, but all he knew was that the victims were varied in age and background, and the first victims were a couple, as far as he remembered.

Did that couple have anything in common with this Horada guy?

When he realized that he didn't know enough about either Horada or the couple to even guess, Yahiro sighed. "In any case, I don't think I'm going to figure out what the culprit is thinking. Do you have any guesses, Himeka?"

"Hmm…well, I can tell you something I heard from a journalist my sister knows… The street attacker's been hitting a lot of delinquents."

"Delinquents?"

"Yes. Nearly half of the victims are members of motorcycle gangs and other people like that. So more and more folks are starting to suspect it has something to do with the street slasher from a few years back."

The street slasher.

That term had popped up in the restaurant just a day or so ago. Yahiro latched on to it. "The slasher… Do you know much about that case, Himeka?"

"I was in middle school at the time, and I hardly ever went out at night…but at school, everybody was being very cautious. From what I've heard, an older girl at our high school was one of the victims…"

"Oh, right. And they never caught who did it…"

Whether it had anything to do with this incident or not, Yahiro figured he might as well learn about that first.

Himeka added, "I think they were called the Dollars… There were some who suspected *them* of being responsible for the slashings… That's probably an area that Kuronuma and his friends would know more about."

♂♀

Ikebukuro

Shouya Ajimura was the street attacker.

But he had no idea.

By day, the twenty-eight-year-old worked small jobs. By night, he was an active fan of *Owl of the Peeping Dead*.

But in this case, his fan works did not mean putting out derivative creative works.

He was an admin of a passionate online community of the most dedicated of *OPD* believers.

He performed a variety of actions around the insular community, agitating the fanatics to keep them united and working in the same direction.

In their minds, their motives were entirely benevolent.

But at times, their activities crossed a line and bled over into causing trouble for others.

For example, one daily routine for them had been to pave the way for *OPD*'s live-action movie to find greater success through review bombing its rivals during the release window.

They also repeatedly told the creative team that "the latest developments lower the quality of *OPD*" and that they were sending "our latest story ideas," which would be "available for use, free of charge."

When there were more new female characters, they wrote in with complaints like, "Stop pandering to gross moe otaku," and when there were more new male characters, the complaints said "Stop pandering to gross *fujoshi*" instead.

When they didn't like the casting for the movie, they decided that "they'll have to switch to a new cast if everyone they signed quits acting." So they sent all kinds of anonymous harassing letters to the actors' agencies by the thousands and spread unsavory rumors all over the Net.

They would describe their offline activities as "playing zombies in the *OPD* Mecca," rampaging around the town like zombies and insulting any normal fans who tried to stop them by saying, "You can't commit to being zombies because you don't really love the series."

That had been happening for so long that the fan site had a rock-bottom reputation, even among *OPD* fans.

Ajimura was the administrator of the site, and he did not care at all about its bad reputation. Those who spoke ill were clearly jealous of the community's size or were haters pretending to be *OPD* fans.

Many of the extreme fans like him prioritized their own love of *OPD* over the material itself.

"Killing your god for the sake of your religion," others said to describe the insular community. Ajimura practically encapsulated this entire statement on his own.

OPD *is written about me.*

The Owl is my good conscience, and the Dark Owl is my negative side.

The zombie apocalypse mirrors my own circumstances. It's brimming with despair.

Maybe they modeled the story after someone just like me.

Maybe they modeled the story after me.

Through this powerful attachment, which quickly crossed into delusion, he began to take mental ownership over the entertainment franchise.

In a way, his "fan activities" were perhaps an attempt to control and rule the world of *OPD*.

In his grand delusion, he believed that ruling the fictional world would therefore extend that control over his own real life. He was already incorrectly assuming the story was based on that line of thinking.

A part of those "fan activities" included cosplaying as the Dark Owl and attacking people on the street.

But he was not *the first* to do so.

When he initially saw the first person on the news, he did not realize the attacker was supposed to resemble the Dark Owl.

It was the online rumors, before the TV and papers caught on, that first spread the information that the attacker was apparently dressed up as the Dark Owl.

When Ajimura noticed, he was shocked.

The Dark Owl was him, *had* to be him—which was how he knew it was wrong. That one was a fake.

Ajimura was furious when he saw the headlines on the tabloids and online articles reading: *Acts of a criminal who cannot tell fact from fiction!*

He thought, *You're wrong. You're wrong, wrong, wrong!*

It's not fiction. OPD is real!

It doesn't belong to anyone else. It's a reality I create for myself alone.

The Dark Owl, a part of that reality, could not be some cheap imitation of a human, who couldn't tell the difference between fact and fiction.

The two things must not be conflated.

"A crime committed under the influence of the story," said a talking head on TV.

Ajimura shouted, "Wrong! You're wrong!"

OPD is my life.

I'm not that cheap and pathetic. No one influenced by me would do something so wretched.

That Dark Owl is wrong. That's not how he's supposed to be depicted!

He shouted more and more for so long that his neighbor started to complain about the noise.

Hours later, he had his face buried into his blanket, thinking furiously.

If the current pattern held true, the public was going to think the Dark Owl was just some irredeemable villain.

Owl of the Peeping Dead was going to be treated like some bible of evil.

His own life was going to be defiled in the court of public opinion.

All those ignorant, arrogant journalists were going to defame him to the world.

So he thought hard and came to a conclusion: *That's it. I have to show them a proper example. I need to teach these ignorant morons what the proper Dark Owl is all about.*

He didn't know *what* he should do. But if he showed it off to the world, the world's opinion of the Dark Owl would be corrected. It had to be.

The next thing he knew, he was shouting something, positively bellowing.

The neighbor was yelling about the noise again.

But this time, Ajimura ignored him, and he yelled and yelled and yelled.

"Goddammit, I told you to shut the hell up! These walls are paper-thin! Your yelling is keepin' me up!"

The next morning, he left his apartment and ran into his neighbor, who grabbed his shirt and voiced his displeasure face-to-face.

Ajimura stood there, his expression lifeless, and thought, *What's his problem?*

The man had dyed hair fashioned into a stylish pompadour. It was very easy to identify him as a delinquent type.

I work hard at a real job. What did I do to deserve being yelled at?

Normally, he might have been terrified into timid obedience, but at this moment, he was at the limit of his frustration, which overwrote his typical reaction with a different one.

"Next time you pull some crap like that, I'm gonna get the landlord to kick you out! Asshole!"

The man left without hitting Ajimura, which was about as peaceful a resolution as could be hoped—except that the insults actually demonstrated to Ajimura a way to justify his Dark Owl.

That's it. It doesn't have to be street attacks. We can say that the Dark Owl was inflicting street justice on the scum of society.

He didn't know who the victims were so far, and he had no interest in them.

But Ajimura knew what should come next.

He knew what he, as the model for the Dark Owl, needed to do.

One night several days later, Ajimura looked at his neighbor, who was lying on the street in the moonless dark evening, bleeding from his head.

And Ajimura thought, *Here we go. No turning back now.*

What arose in his heart was not fear but elation.

At this moment, he was finally one and the same with the Dark Owl.

However…

The problem was that in the actual story, *the Dark Owl was not some crusader of justice who only hunted the wicked.*

It was the kind of misconception that would earn you scorn from ordinary fans like Yumasaki and Karisawa. "You're not a real fan!" they would shout. In fact, Ajimura's site was known to them as the kind of place fans weren't meant to go—it was even nastier and more toxic than a hotbed of haters.

But at this point, the difference between Ajimura's conception of the character and its actual depiction in *OPD* was immaterial. *OPD* was his life, and it was the series that would be corrected to match *him*, he believed.

The truth was, while he worked up the crowd on the fan site, he had only ever skimmed the *OPD* anime. He'd never even bought the DVDs or manga volumes.

It was his life, after all, so why did he need to wholly consume it?

And after attacking his neighbor, there was truly nothing holding his mind in place anymore.

He observed the local thugs, anticipated their behavioral patterns, and attacked them late at night when no one was watching.

But although he was only selecting people that society termed *scum* for elimination, the TV was still calling his actions "random street attacks."

"It's not enough. I haven't gotten enough of them; that's why they don't understand yet," Ajimura muttered to himself in the convenience store where he worked, eyeing the group of street toughs hanging out in the parking lot outside.

"The guy named Horada was just a nobody... They're not even raising a fuss about this online... I need to do more. Need to hunt worse scumbags. Time to wipe out all the trolls..."

He needed to find famous scumbugs. The kind of people that he would be a hero for eliminating.

On his break, Ajimura searched for fresh information on his smartphone.

He ran a search on the keywords *Tokyo delinquent famous*. One name popped up above all.

It was a name he recognized.

If you were a young person and you lived in the vicinity of Ikebukuro, you probably knew that name.

After all, alongside the Headless Rider, he was one of the most famous legends of Ikebukuro.

Drops of cold sweat beaded on Ajimura's forehead, and his eyes were brimming with intention.

"Shizuo...Heiwajima..."

♂♀

Shinra's apartment

"Look for the attacker? You?" Shinra squawked.

By his nature, Shinra did not inquire into the contents of Celty's job, but when she asked him, *"Have you heard any new stories about the street attacker?"* it became clear to him what she'd been working on for the last few days.

"Yeah, there's a new odd jobs place called Snake Hands, and I'm looking for information on the street attacker for them."

"That's dangerous, Celty! What if you get hurt by this attacker?"

"You used to say the same thing when I started working as a courier..."

"Well, I've managed to accept the courier job as something you wanted to do for yourself, but I really worry that this suspicious Snake Hands group is just using you for their own benefit. Are those kids treating you like some kind of convenient weapon or armor? It's just like Aoba," Shinra said with great concern.

Celty tilted her helmet in a nod. *"It's fine. I treat it like a business, and I'm not doing anything unless it's for the right price. Besides, getting smacked with a hammer isn't going to do anything to me..."*

"Well, if you say so...," he said, seemingly satisfied.

After all the wild events of the past, Shinra largely stayed out of Celty's business when she was getting herself into danger. It was in cases like this, where she got involved on someone *else's* request, that he got worried.

Most likely, he was less worried about her getting hurt and more worried about her being manipulated into some situation that she didn't want to be in.

Celty understood that, too, which is why she added some information meant to put Shinra at ease.

"Plus, my clients in this case are Yumasaki and Karisawa. In a way, that makes me feel reassured about the job."

"Those two? Why them?" he asked, confused once again, so Celty told him about what she'd heard from Kuon.

"Uh-huh... Well, that clears it up... I had no idea that was going on with the street attacks. I never knew because I haven't been following the news these days."

"You only pay attention to articles about me."

"Of course, Celty! Even setting aside that horrible fake news about you having a damned boyfriend, people everywhere are getting worked up about you coming back to town! I feel proud—it's like a member of the family turning into a celebrity."

"Uh...it's more like becoming famous for being a criminal. That's not something to be proud of."

Naturally, Celty was working as a courier, which meant she was riding around without headlights or a license plate. She felt guilty whenever someone praised her for her job activities.

Shinra noticed that she was feeling self-conscious, so he changed the topic. "Anyway...people getting attacked on the street? It reminds me of all that stuff around Anri."

"Yes, I suppose that's right. That was a street slasher. This one's more of a bludgeoner. It feels rather strange."

"Speaking of Anri, how is Sonohara-dou doing these days?" he asked.

That put Celty in a good mood. *"Business is brisk, it seems. Masaomi and Saki have been going all over Japan and acquiring things to sell there. Their selection is much richer than you'd imagine."*

Celty thought of Anri like a little sister, and her mind drifted to her from time to time ever since the girl had graduated from Raira Academy.

Celty kept up an e-mail correspondence with her, as she did with Mikado, although she met Anri in person much less often, to keep her out of the turbulent and dangerous underworld. When Anri found herself in possession of some strange or suspicious artifact, Celty was available to offer her thoughts on it.

"Apparently, that Kujiragi woman brings her stuff from time to time, too... She might have a real talent for assembling a bizarre inventory."

"Ah, yes... Kujiragi seems like the type to bring in weird stuff to sell. Speaking of which, wasn't she on the run from the police?"

"Your dad's a regular customer, too. He pops his head in every time he comes back to Japan."

"Ah…well, hopefully he's not interfering with her business…" Shinra traced his cheek as he envisioned a man with a creepy white gas mask visiting an antiques seller.

"Well…I suppose it's possible that the street attacks are coming from a curse like Saika…"

Saika was the name of Anri's cursed katana. At one time, the curse had plunged Ikebukuro into fear of mysterious, indiscriminate slashings, but that was now a chapter of the past.

"Speaking of which, aren't you holding on to Saika for Kujiragi? What happened with that?"

"Oh, I've still got it. I agreed to give it back the next time we meet; it just hasn't happened yet."

"…Does it feel to you like she's going to leave it with you forever…?"

"You think so? Speaking of which, I haven't checked up on it since we came back from our trip," Shinra said, getting to his feet and opening up the cabinet that contained his medical tools.

Inside was a long, thin item wrapped in cloth, which he brought out in view of Celty.

"You just had it hanging out in there?!"

He undid the cloth to reveal a blade transformed into a scalpel. When he picked it up, his eyes glowed red.

Saika.

A cursed sword with a will of its own that had been handed down in Edo through the ages. In modern Japan, there were several confirmed Saikas, in fact.

The blade apparently held a woman's personality within it and possessed the strange aspect of a desire to "love" all of humanity.

When the sword cut a person, its "words of love" would invade the victim's body through the wound, eating away at their mind, until they had become a "child" of Saika, a puppet for the blade's user to control.

That wielder, too, unless they possessed an exceptionally strong will, would be taken over by Saika and existed as a manifestation of her love, attacking other people to spread it further.

Whoever possessed Saika had glowing red eyes while using it, and the wounded children had bloodshot eyes as well. Whatever bladed object they held was used to cut more people, creating grandchildren. This was the danger that Saika posed to humanity.

In the past, Shinra had been turned into a child of Saika and ultimately conquered his curse. Now he owned one of the parent Saikas.

And at the moment, his eyes were gleaming like red LEDs, demonstrating his ownership.

"See? Real, right?"

"H-hey, are you sure about this?! What if the accursed voice gets...?"

"Yeah, it's real annoying while I'm holding it, but as long as I'm looking at your face, I don't mind it," Shinra said with a grin. He started wrapping up the scalpel again.

Once she saw his eyes returning to their normal color, Celty felt relieved. *"You were really taking your life into your own hands back then..."*

"Hey, it worked out, didn't it? And you be careful, all right? If anything happens to you, I'll have no choice but to make the lives of all the people who did it to you into a living hell. Heh-heh-heh-heh."

"Don't be ominous," she warned; it was exactly the sort of thing she thought he would do.

If something did happen to her, it was likely to involve Shinra, too, by the sheer nature of things.

For one thing, Shinra was the type of person who liked taking walks at night, so there was no guarantee he couldn't be one of the attacker's victims.

She wanted to catch the attacker no matter what to keep Shinra safe—but out of shyness or some other reason, she hadn't told him that directly.

Shinra's phone lit up with an incoming call.

"Hmm, I wonder who this could be so late at night... Ah, it's Shizuo," he said and quickly pressed the button to accept the call. "Hello? What do you want at this hour?"

"Did something happen, I wonder?" Celty wrote to Shinra as he waited for the answer. She listened closely for the voice on the other end. Although she couldn't make out the words, the sound of Shizuo's voice told her that he was in a rather agitated state.

"All right. We'll leave the door unlocked. Come right up the elevator," Shinra said. The tension was heightened in his voice, too. That told Celty that it was something big.

"What's up?" she asked him once he'd ended the call.

Shinra returned the scalpel-type Saika to the cabinet and began to pull out disinfectants and other chemicals instead.

"Go and unlock the door, Celty. Shizuo's going to bring a patient up here."

"Someone's hurt?!"

"Yes. I think you know him, too. His coworker, Tanaka? The man with the dreads and glasses," Shinra said.

"It seems Tanaka got attacked on the street, and they banged his head pretty bad..."

INTERMISSION
Online Rumors

On the Ikebukuro information site IkeNew! Version I.KEBU.KUR.O

New Post: A civic group announced they want the *Owl of the Peeping Dead* movie and anime canceled!

→Those PC Bloodbags who were already coming out hard against *OPD* just made a formal announcement. If this picks up momentum, it's going to end up censoring not just the manga but the movie as well.

→These Bloodbags are wild. They're claiming that the Headless Rider, the Night of the Ripper, and even the recent faked group kidnapping were all caused by the influence of anime, movies, and manga—especially *OPD*. The freakin' Headless Rider has been in Ikebukuro for over twenty years!

→So it's finally come to this. That civic group is famous for being wackos, but they've got political connections, too. Let's just hope this doesn't lead to new restrictions on artistic expression.

→The same group previously said that a yakuza movie based in Ikebukuro was "glorifying violent mob groups like the Awakusu-kai" and tried to sue to stop it from being sold. It's like, which one of us is having trouble distinguishing reality from fiction?

(Selected from comments on Twittia)

Excerpt from a public speech:

"...You see, our children are pure and innocent, and they cannot be expected to know which books and visuals are appropriate for them. Therefore, it falls to sensible adults like us to protect our children from these owls and their deadly ilk. In order to clear the air we breathe in Ikebukuro and take back the public health of our city, we must push for restrictions of certain items being sold in the anime shops and book-stores of Ikebukuro... The lawless individual they call the Headless Rider is clearly motivated by the influence of corrupting video games, and anyone can see that incidents like the street slasher are the effect of violent manga, anime, movies, and music... This WWW group has clearly made a deal with the devil. They are destroying Ikebukuro, and in a sense, they're even more diabolical than the attacker who contin-ues to inflict damage on our people. WWW has created a story that fills Ikebukuro with corpses, and we must insist that every product bearing this property is confiscated at once. If they will not listen, then the honorable citizens of Ikebukuro must raise their fists and deliver a righteous blow to these preachers of heresy. It may be righteous, but it is not divine. We will fight for ourselves to protect our children's future and our right to a live in a virtuous, decent Ikebukuro..."

Comment from IkeNew! *Administrator*

The PC Bloodbags have gone off theiw wockers again. They may be officiawwy cawed People for the Calm Treatment of Ikebukuro, but this merely abbreviates to P.C.T.I.BUKURO. With *ti* (*chi*) meaning "blood" and *bukuro* meaning "bag," evewyone just cawws dem PC Bloodbags.

You know, if they're not careful, that part at the end about "delivering a righteous blow" could be seen as a thweat. I mean, not that it's a stretch to reach that concwusion.

It's scawwy. It's fweaky!

The stweet attackew's scawwy, but so are the thugs forming up new gangs.

God save us aww.

Admin: Rira Tailtooth Zaiya

♂♀

That stupid IkeNew guy put my twits in his article without permission again.

→They won't listen to whatever you say. Just gotta deal with it.

→I've given up on stopping them. It just pisses me off that he gets affiliate money on his blog.

→The thing is, IkeNew's still one of the better ones.

→I just hate how that stupid admin writes.

Wow, look at all those anime nerds getting triggered. This is the perfect chance to mass report any user whining about the civic group and get them kicked off Twittia, right?

→STFU and die.

→Well, well, it took less than a minute for the anime avatars to descend upon me lolol

→This guy sucks. Look, I screenshotted all his past stupid twits.

→Hmm? Why would you collect all my twits? I've reported you for doxing lol

→Thanks.

→Huh?

→OMG he actually did it.

→I can't believe he actually reported it.

→When you report a twit to Twittia, the other person can see your name and address, man.

→Wait, what?

→Says here you live in *** Prefecture? They're famous for their textiles, aren't they?

→What do you mean? No way, this can't be happening!

→Calm down, Mr. ***. I'll give you a call later lmao

You know, I saw someone I think was the attacker yesterday. They were running away down Kawagoe Highway.

→Really? I didn't see anything about that in the news.

→Hmm. Well, there was someone bleeding from their head at a nearby convenience store.

→Holy shit.

→Yeah, there was a guy in a bartender's getup carrying him off to see a doctor.

→Bartender...? Was he blond, wearing shades?

→Uh, yeah. I dunno about the shades, but he was blond.

→That street attacker's as good as dead.

I gotta wonder what this attacker wants, you know?

→Just to attack people, right?

→Nah, it kinda feels like the victims alternate between punks and normal people.

→Sure it's not random?

→ If every other person who gets whacked is a thug, it should clean up Ikebukuro pretty quick…

→ I bet the thugs are just being made out to look like the street attacker's work.

→ The Night of the Ripper was weird like that, too. Over fifty in one night.

→ No way that was just one person's work…

→ Probably the Dollars, I bet.

→ The Dollars! Remember them? lol

If the PC Bloodbags have enough time on their hands to crack down on manga, I wish they'd do something about the actual street gang remnants still kicking around.

→ Dragon Zombie's been riding a bunch these days… Though a lot get arrested by traffic cops.

→ No Yellow Scarves, though… Are there any color gangs anymore?

→ I think there are a few Blue Squares here and there.

→ They're sooo behind the times. Can't they just go away?

→ And the Headless Rider's back, too.

→ Why don't we just blame the street attacks and everything on the Dollars?

→ I wonder what the Dollars are doing now?

→ Yeah, it'd be really embarrassing to go around calling yourself "former Dollars"…

CHAPTER
3

CHAPTER 3
Protect Our Ikebukuro

Why doesn't anyone understand?

I've caused so much harm, and yet there are still fools out there who coddle that stupid, vulgar manga. The mass media roll over on their bellies like weaklings.

It's the movie. This all started because there's a movie.

They'll willingly bash a manga or an anime, but when there's a live-action movie involved, you've got high-profile actors and their powerful talent agencies, don't you? Or maybe it's because the TV networks and major ad agencies are in on the business.

The problem is, this is exactly the moment to stop letting those worldly concerns control us. Don't they get it?

I haven't done enough yet.

How much more must I do to make them understand?

When will they realize how dangerous that awful devil is?

But I can't stop now. I can't.

I sold my soul to the devil for this.

I sold my soul to the devil to warn them *about* the devil.

I sold out.

♂♀

Shinra's apartment

"Oooh, owww. This was hell, man."

Sighing, Tom Tanaka rubbed softly at the bandages wrapped around his head.

"Just to be on the safe side, I'd recommend going to a hospital in the morning for an X-ray and a CT scan," Shinra advised.

Tom bobbed his head as he put his glasses on. "You've done me a real solid, doc. Sorry for barging in on you in the middle of the night like this."

"You feelin' okay, Tom?" asked Shizuo, eyeing the bandages.

Tom waved his hand. "Yeah, I'll be fine. It was a close call, though."

From what he said, Tom was attacked on the street not far away during the night.

He'd been collecting on people's debts for his job—the usual—and after successfully collecting from a target who'd returned home at a late hour, he was attacked.

Shizuo was inside the convenience store, trying to choose between cartons of caramel- or vanilla-flavored café au lait. Tom, who'd already finished his purchase, was drinking a can of coffee in the parking lot next to the building when the assailant struck.

In fact, Tom noticed the attacker in the nick of time and just barely dodged the hammer's blow, but the reaction caused him to lose his balance. He toppled over a bicycle and against a public phone, banging his forehead on the hard corner of the attached phone book. That's how he started bleeding.

Shizuo went outside to find out what was going on. Tom watched the attacker in black pajamas leap over the wall behind the store. Shizuo rushed over to help Tom immediately, and that was how the attacker managed to get away.

"I saw them running away, too…but Tom's head was bleeding, and I was worried. That was enough time for them to escape… I figured you were closer than the hospital, so that's why I called. Sorry for the disturbance," said Shizuo, looking solemn.

Celty typed, *"When you said he'd been attacked, I just assumed he got hit with a hammer."*

"Nah, if he took a shot like that, he might've even died. It was wrapped up in bandages or something like that, but I'm pretty sure it was a hammer."

"That would certainly point to the ever-popular street attacker," Shinra noted, showing them a picture from the Internet. It was a still of the Dark Owl character from the *Owl of the Peeping Dead* anime. "Is this the one who attacked you?"

"Y-yeah," Tom said, sounding a bit uncomfortable. He glanced back at Shizuo.

Behind his shades, Shizuo's brows were clearly knitted. "What do you mean, street attacker?" he asked Shinra.

Celty tilted her helmet. *Huh? Does Shizuo…not know about the street attacker? I know he's not the type to dig into TV or online news, but I would have figured that his coworker Tom here would've mentioned it in passing, at least.*

And for some reason, based on Shizuo's reaction, Shinra made a face like he was thinking, *Oh, crap.*

While Celty waited in confusion, Shinra let a few seconds of awkward silence pass before he began to describe the string of incidents in a very roundabout way.

"Okay… I see what's going on," Shizuo muttered to himself several minutes later, once Shinra's story was done. Then he said, "Well, you've been a huge help, Shinra. Thanks a lot."

"Uh, sure. Don't worry about it. I know I owe you a few favors, at the very least." Shinra's forehead was sweaty. He looked and sounded awkward.

Shizuo turned on his heel. "I should be off now. Take care of Tom for me."

"Huh? Go where?" Shinra asked.

"Hmph. Where else?" He chuckled to himself, then looked dead serious. "I'm gonna find the attacker who hurt Tom, and I'm gonna *pound them into dust.*"

Into dust?!

A nasty shiver ran down both Shinra and Celty's spines.

Shizuo's voice was strangely calm, but that was just a sign he was holding it in.

Holding in his rage.

It was a kind of calmness he demonstrated when there was no present target for his fury. In the past, in this very room, just after learning that he'd been taken advantage of by Izaya Orihara, he gave Akane Awakusu a shockingly plucky smile. This situation felt very similar.

"Uh, Shinra, do you think Shizuo's this mad because his coworker was attacked?" Celty typed, discreetly showing him her smartphone screen.

Shinra whispered back, "Yes, that's half of it."

"? What's the other half?"

"Umm...well...I guess you didn't know, then..." Shinra looked away, then shrugged and said, "So you know that Dark Owl?"

"The character?"

"He's played by Yuuhei in the movie."

"...Huh?"

Celty's mind went completely blank.

"During our hot spring vacation, we didn't go see any movies, and you don't look at movie websites or Yuuhei's fan sites, do you? He appeared as a kind of surprise guest, without any publicity ahead of time. His face doesn't show up in the movie, and it's a surprise, so his name value doesn't add anything, but their agency president thought it was funny, so he signed off on it."

"Yuuhei, like...Yuuhei Hanejima?"

"Yes, exactly. Shizuo's younger brother."

Yuuhei Hanejima. Real name, Kasuka Heiwajima.

He was Shizuo Heiwajima's brother and one of the hottest young actors in the business.

That explained the earlier concern.

Tom was careful not to talk about the street attacker around Shizuo. Given that his brother, Yuuhei, was in the movie and *playing* the very character whom the attacker was cosplaying as, it was obvious what would result if he found out. Out of an abundance of caution, Tom made sure never to let Shizuo come into contact with that information.

Unfortunately, that concern was well-founded, especially when Tom's victimization only made the overall payoff *more* serious. The total mass of Shizuo's pure, violent rage toward the attacker was all the greater.

Oh no, someone's going to die. The attacker's earned it, but he really is going to pound them into dust! Celty panicked.

Shinra said, "Uh, hold on, Shizuo. How are you going to search for this attacker?"

"Huh...? I just look for someone wearing those clothes, then grind them to a pulp on the asphalt, obviously..."

"I wasn't asking *how* you were going to turn them into dust! Plus, what you're describing is mincemeat, not dust!" Shinra insisted, arguing a pointless distinction.

From behind him, Tom called out, "Hey, Shizuo. It won't work. There are a bunch of people wearing those pajamas."

"...? What do you mean?" Shizuo asked.

"Oh, right, right," interjected Shinra. "Ever since the attacks started, people have been buying tons of those onesies for fun. I'm not sure if they're just trying to mess with the police, but the fact is, there are a fair number of folks walking around in them. Right, Celty?"

"Yeah...I wouldn't say you see them all over...but they're around here and there."

"...Now that you mention it, I guess I probably have seen them, too...," Shizuo muttered as he placed his hand against the wall. "But... on the other hand, whether they think it's a fun game or what, walking around town with misleading clothes on like that is kind of a threat to other folks, isn't it? Someone might even get startled and die from a heart attack, you know? And that means those folks should be prepared to get pounded into dust, yeah...?"

"Hold on, hold on! Relax, Shizuo!" Celty typed frantically, trying to calm Shizuo before his mind started going down that dark path.

What a disaster. He was finally starting to chill out! And that stupid street attacker! They just had to go and do this...

It almost made her wonder if the culprit had a death wish. She continued typing.

"The police are out there searching all over for this guy and so am I. So can you let us do our job?"

*   *   *

Ultimately, after a long, desperate attempt by Celty, Tom, and Shinra to talk Shizuo down, the clincher was Tom saying, "Look, I don't wanna be the cause of you raising hell around the hood, and I bet your brother doesn't, either." That was just enough to get Shizuo to stifle his rage.

"…All right. I guess I'll stay put for today, for you and Celty…"

"Huh? What about me? *Urmmmg…*"

Shinra was in the process of inserting himself unnecessarily when Celty stuffed his mouth with shadow.

"I'm glad to hear it. For now, just focus on getting Tom home safely."

"That's a good idea. Thanks, Celty," Shizuo said. He gave her a piercing stare, then came out with a request of his own.

"But if you *do* find that guy, *you'll let me know before anyone else…* right?"

"Huh?"

"You said you're lookin' for the attacker, right?"

Oh, shoot.

"Uh, yeah."

"So if you find him before the cops do, I just wanna talk with him."

"That might be, uh…"

"Don't worry—I just want to talk to him. I'm sure he's got some real good reasons for what he's done…"

His rage was smoldering deep in his chest, but not on the surface—yet.

"Uh, I'll see what I can do," Celty replied noncommittally, hearing the endless, murderous fury in Shizuo's voice. She walked him and Tom to the door.

As they left, Tom whispered to her, "Sorry about this. I'll calm him down over time." That was a relief, and once they were gone, Celty wilted and sat down in the middle of the hallway.

"Are you all right, Celty?"

"Yeah…thanks, Shinra. I'm fine," she wrote, but deeper down, she was a mess of panic and confusion. *"If he finds out that I let Yumasaki's group meet the attacker before him, I feel like we're going to suffer because of it.*

* * *

"What am I going to do if I actually catch the attacker...?"

♂♀

Raira Academy library—next morning

The weeklong holiday headed into its second half, and Yahiro found himself at school on the weekend, volunteering to help organize the shelves at the library.

About a third of the library committee were there, perhaps because they didn't have anything else to do. They hustled back and forth between the librarians' room and the shelves.

There was less to do than anticipated, and they might actually finish up before noon. Yahiro came to a stop and took a break, using the time to speak to the library chairman.

"Ummm, excuse me..."

"Hi there, Mizuchi. What's up?"

"Um...are you familiar with the street slasher incident?"

"...Why, yes. It happened after I started at this school," the chairman replied, smiling amiably.

"Well, there's this street attacker now, you know?" Yahiro continued. "I'm just wondering...do you think the same person is behind the attacks?"

"Hmm. Why do you say that?"

"I think it would be frightening to get attacked like that, so I was thinking it over...," Yahiro said. He hesitated, then continued clearly, "I get the feeling...that there's not just one attacker."

"Why do you say that?"

"...Maybe this doesn't make any sense, but I've been thinking about my plan if the attacker comes after me, and I was looking up information from other incidents...and I can't narrow it down to one plan. There's always some weird disconnect there in the fine details..."

Despite the lack of confidence in Yahiro's description, the older boy seemed to find it interesting. He opened the window and asked, "When you say plan...do you mean what you'll do if you get attacked?"

"Uh, yes. Maybe that's a strange thing to do."

"Not at all. It's never a bad thing to prepare. But I think the best plan of all is not walking around after dark."

That was such an obvious and effective piece of advice that Yahiro could say nothing. In fact, it made him feel just a bit guilty, because he was actually *trying* to get closer to the attacker.

"And what connection do you suspect this has to the slasher?" the chairman asked.

"Oh, right. Apparently, there are rumors out there that the slasher was actually a group of people...and there are some who theorize that it was part of some kind of gang war. Between groups called the Dollars and Yellow Scarves... Do you know much about that?"

"A little," the chairman said with a smile.

Yahiro hypothesized, "What if there's some group that's not all on the same page, like the Dollars, and they're working in separate groups toward some goal? In that case, it would make sense that their methods aren't all in alignment..."

"Maybe they're *not* working toward the same goal."

"Huh?" Yahiro yelped, taken aback by this suggestion.

The library chairman dusted off the stack of books on the desk by the window. "What if there were multiple street attackers with completely different intentions? Forget about which one came first and which was the copycat. If they keep working toward their separate intentions, it makes sense that you wouldn't be able to narrow it down to the work of one distinct person."

"Uh-huh... That's a good point."

"I'm pretty sure the police have been on to that idea for a while, though. For one thing, the victims are heavily weighted toward street hooligans."

"Oh, my friend said that, too," Yahiro said, recalling his conversation with Himeka. He could feel his thoughts getting clearer.

"Right. The attacker going after those hooligans and the attacker going after everyone else can be pretty easily separated into two, I think. So what would happen to the confusion in your mind if you made distinct plans for those two sides?"

"......"

Yahiro looked at his smartphone to confirm the information he'd saved there, then began to simulate what he would do if he was attacked on the street again. As a result—at least, as far as the delinquent-attacking group was concerned—the actions of the attacker lined up, giving him a path to a counterplan that he found satisfactory.

"…Thank you. I'll think more about this."

"Thinking things over is all well and good, but don't go getting yourself into danger, okay?" the chairman said with a smile, closing the window. He seemed to be able to see right through Yahiro.

The younger boy bowed in thanks, right as the bell rang to indicate that break time was over.

"Oh, there it goes. It's weird to hear the school bell on a day without class, isn't it?" the older student said. As Yahiro headed back to work, he called out, "There's one thing you don't need to worry about, though: This doesn't have anything to do with the slasher."

"Huh? Okay."

Yahiro wasn't exactly sure how that was supposed to make him worry less, but then he decided that the fact that this one didn't have a blade was something to be relieved about.

As he rushed off, drawing his own conclusions, the chairman grimaced and added, "At least, that's the hunch I get."

After Yahiro left, the library chairman turned back to the window and sighed.

Through his uniform, Mikado Ryuugamine rubbed at the stab wound scars on his stomach and murmured to himself, "I hardly ever hear the voice anymore…but it does still have an effect on my eyes."

He looked into the reflection of his eyes on the window glass and grinned. It started off as more of a pained grimace, but in time, it turned into an expression of honest relief.

By taking on the curse of Saika, he was able to detect how active the presence of that curse was within the city.

The stabbing came at the hands of a man possessed by Saika, and it caused the curse to flow into him. It was barely a glimmer of what it once was, but he could still use it to sense others like him.

And when the presence in the city dimmed and he was able to confirm that the people he cared about weren't involved in these street attacks, he felt a great amount of relief.

It seemed to tell him that as long as he knew that much, he wouldn't need to venture into the underworld of the city again.

As Yahiro returned to the library shelves, he thought about the chairman.

I kind of feel like Ryuugamine's eyes were really bloodshot just now... I wonder if he was hard at work before we showed up. I should help out more...

He headed back to his work—both the duties of his library committee and the Snake Hands work after that.

He'd been very close to the lingering echo of the abnormal, but he had no idea it was even there.

♂♀

Raira General Hospital, private room

"Are you all right, Mr. Horada?" asked Aoba, grinning widely.

Horada's cheek twitched. "Y-yeah. Doin' just grand."

"I'm shocked, though. Where's this 'find the attacker' stuff coming from? You just finished getting questioned by the police, so I assumed you were going to leave it up to them."

Horada found the younger member of the Blue Squares oddly intimidating, but he decided that it had to be an illusion of Izumii, the boy's older brother. He shook his head to clear the fear away.

"Yeow!"

The shaking caused the pain to double back on him. He slumped back onto the bed.

"What's the matter?"

"N-nothin'," he said, and to hide his pain, he answered Aoba's earlier question with more force than was needed. "Listen, I used to be the face of the Blue Squares! If I pull back now, that's my name as a man that gets tarnished! Am I wrong?"

"Well, you might have a point..."

"Don't worry. I got some deets I didn't tell the cops."

"Really?!" Aoba exclaimed.

Horada beamed with satisfaction at that, feeling some measure of superiority through the younger boy's shock.

The information he did not share with the police was that there were two attackers. He'd told them it was one person who did this to him. None of the eyewitness information mentioned two attackers, and if some discrepancy turned up, he could always say his memory was shaky on account of being hit.

Izumii told him to finish it up before the cops did, so he figured lying to them would help throw them off the proper trail.

Uh...but...what do I say? Sayin' only two of them ganged up on me kinda makes me sound like a bitch...

After a bit of thought, Horada's innate smallness of character shone through, and he ended up embellishing the story by quite a lot.

"So, uh...I knocked out the first two or three, like you know I'd do..."

"Huh?"

"But when there's more than five, even I can't last forever, so..."

"..."

Aoba considered this revelation gravely. Upon seeing the reaction, Horada inwardly cursed himself.

Aw, shit. Did I go too far?! Should have kept it to three... What kinda street attacker has over five people? That's just a buncha violent thugs ambushing innocent people!

It was remarkable how much that image exactly matched Horada and his underlings and what they were used to doing, but he was incapable of being self-aware. Instead, he waited nervously to see how Aoba would react.

Once he was sure that Aoba had seen right through him, he was stunned to hear the boy say, "So you mean...it was a group of them?"

"Huh? Uh, y-yeah. That's what I'm sayin', see? There's no way I'd get decked by some random asshole on the street! And I didn't even tell the cops that...so be careful you don't spread that, yeah?"

"Got it. I'll make sure the police don't hear about it."

"Uh...cool."

Aoba took the news so smoothly that it creeped Horada out a little, until he reconsidered.

There we go. Good little boy believes what he hears. Real easy to fool. Guess it's just a sign of how well I'm respected.

Rather optimistically, he assumed that it was due to his natural charisma.

But he had no idea what kind of ideas were floating through Aoba's mind.

♂♀

A few minutes later, outside the hospital

"Yo, Aoba. How's our big buddy doing?" asked one of his friends, who'd been waiting outside the building.

"Hmm…things are trickier than I thought," he replied gravely.

"What do you mean?"

"I had a feeling that there was more than one attacker…but I didn't think they would actually team up on a single target."

"Huh?"

Aoba proceeded to tell them what he'd heard from Horada.

"…And that's what he said."

"Is that for real? He wasn't just talkin' bullshit? He looks like he would." His friends were skeptical.

Aoba's response was measured. "If he wanted the attackers caught for his own sake, he wouldn't have needed to make up a bunch of nonsense. And he seems terrified of my brother, so I can't see him trying to make use of us just to protect his own image."

But Aoba didn't know that his very brother, Ran Izumii, had given Horada his orders already. He was having difficulty pinning down Horada's personal nature.

"He's a weird guy, I guess. Like, it's clear that he's chickenshit, but some of the things he does go way beyond my expectations. I can't even guess how he found the hideout of that faked mass kidnapping…"

Unfortunately, for Aoba, the truth was frustratingly out of his grasp—that it was sheer coincidence. And that lack of clarity made Horada's full portrait more eerie and mysterious by the day.

Based on his appearance and words, he was just a small-time coward who tried to play a big man. In fact, during the takeover of the Yellow Scarves a few years ago, he was nothing more than another face in the Blue Squares lineup who was more than happy to dance in the palm of Aoba's hand, but...

Did something happen while he was in prison? Maybe something's going on behind my back.

Perhaps because he had such a two-sided personality, Aoba suspected that Horada might be a kindred spirit in that regard. He was plagued by illusions that there must be *some* reason or some mysterious happenings going on in the dark.

"It's like his natural cowardice is camouflage. It might be his true weapon, in fact."

"What's 'camouflage'?"

"Look it up."

Aoba walked off toward the exit of the hospital grounds, considering the latest developments.

He had a fairly good idea of who was responsible, but the fact that multiple people had attacked Horada added a different meaning to the mix.

If there were multiple attackers with separate goals, did that mean—at worst—that there was a group of people with the same goal in mind?

Perhaps a cruel-intentioned group of thugs were the copycat, eliminating their rivals by ganging up on them, one at a time.

"Well, damn. This isn't quite what I expected it to be." He pulled out his phone and began to write a text message.

"Who you texting, man?" one of his friends asked.

"The Headless Rider."

"What?"

His friend's eyebrows shot up, much to Aoba's delight.

"Gotta call in that favor for sending her a photo of Himeka Tatsugami, after all," he said and hit the send button.

The message itself was quite simple—but embellished here and there, intended to worry its recipient.

Hi, Celty.
This is Aoba.
Sorry this is coming out of nowhere, but could you help with finding this attacker who's got Ikebukuro on edge?

If you find them, we'd really appreciate you bringing them to us.

I'm thinking it's possible that there are actually dozens of people conducting these attacks.

It might turn out to be a return of the Night of the Ripper.

♂♀

Shinra's apartment

"What the heck is this?!"

Celty showed her complaint to Shinra and flopped dramatically onto the couch.

"What's that? Can you show me the message?" Shinra asked, taking her phone and checking the most recent message she'd received. Before he even saw the text, the sight of the name Aoba Kuronuma put a very displeased look on his face.

"Oh…"

"Even Aoba's talking about the attacker, and he says it might turn out like the Night of the Ripper! What am I supposed to do about that? What does he mean, there might be dozens of them?!"

"You don't think there's something at play like that cursed sword, do you…?"

"What do you mean? First a cursed sword, now a cursed hammer?!" Celty's frustration came in loud and clear even over text.

"I've heard of such a thing," Shinra said gravely. "A wicked, cursed hammer by the name of Bannanjin that possesses people and causes their desires to accelerate out of control. Perhaps that's what we're dealing with…"

"No! Stop! Don't make this any worse!"

"Well, setting that aside, you should see this as a good thing, Celty. If there are multiple attackers, you can give one to Shizuo and the rest to Yumasaki and Karisawa. Or save the leftovers for Aoba."

"We're not talking about vacation souvenirs here!" Celty snapped, but her annoyance helped center her, and she sat up on the sofa. *"What does it mean if there really are more than one? Do you think some motorcycle gang is involved?"*

"I'm not sure. Maybe after all the fuss the media's making about it, someone's getting influenced and playing along."

"Like a copycat, you mean...?"

That made a certain kind of sense to Celty, and she tried to imagine who would commit a copycat attack.

Someone who saw the attacker story on the news and decided they wanted to be part of it. In any case, it's not someone with a good head on their shoulders...and it might not even be a grown-up.

"Well, I bet it's just some young airheaded clique or a delinquent student..."

♂♀

Youko Shirobishi was the street attacker.

She was fully aware of this.

She understood that what she was doing was evil, but she believed that it was for the purpose of doing good.

So she was certain that her actions were forgivable and that someone else ought to bear the punishment. And therefore, she continued to beat strangers on the street.

Youko was a thirty-seven-year-old self-described essayist who uploaded her writings to the Internet, but the income her site made through ad banners was just a few thousand yen per year. She survived by eating through the inheritance her parents left her.

There were no offerings to them on the Buddhist altar in her home. In fact, they seemed to stare balefully out at the room from their framed photograph there, gathering dust.

She did not care about any of that in the slightest. She believed that she was living for a much higher, nobler cause.

Harmony.

World harmony.

Temporal harmony.

Her life was spent in pursuit of a beautiful world where all things existed in perfect accord. That meant she could not let herself be occupied with personal concerns like cleaning up the altar for her late parents.

This was her actual thought process, and she saw everything, from honoring her parents to cleaning her room, as the kind of worldly concern to be ignored. Instead, she fought against an illogical world with her words as weapons.

Even the few thousand yen in ad banner revenue was mostly due to her site going viral—in a bad way.

When she attacked something that disrupted harmony, she tended to attract the attention of those who were drawn to the corruption of nature and the world—she wrote on her website. But put more simply, she was merely picking fights with everyone she could.

And when curious onlookers came by to check out the fuss, a small number of them clicked on her ad banners, making her a pittance.

Anything she described as "disrupting harmony" was, in short, something that disrupted people's tranquility.

That disruption could be agitation, fear, anger, laziness, desire—anything that caused the emotional needle to swing back and forth.

Manga with intense sexual depictions qualified, of course, as did horror movies with extreme violence, police dramas with gunfights, even works of fine art that featured the nude form. All these things were her enemies.

An especially rich example of her controversies was when she attempted to get pictures of the Venus de Milo banned from textbooks for being "violently sexist art spreading the ideology that a woman is more beautiful when her arms are ripped off."

Different theories exist about whether the statue originally had arms that crumbled off or if it had been made without arms to begin with, but to Youko, this distinction did not matter in the least. The fact that it existed as a piece of art to be appreciated disgusted her. She considered it an act of blasphemy against society.

If that was her attitude toward ancient works of art, it was no surprise that she was brutally aggressive toward modern TV shows, comics, and movies. And foremost among her targets was a media franchise by the name of *Owl of the Peeping Dead*.

It was a story in which zombies take over Ikebukuro and the living have to find a way to survive—but Youko's reaction toward the premise went past disgust and into a kind of primordial terror.

For one thing, she was completely incapable of understanding the concept of zombies that come back to life and attack people.

If a child watches this, who is going to teach them that people don't *actually keep moving after you kill them?* she wondered, aghast. She'd been a member of a civil group that attempted to purge all zombie movies out of concern, but her methods were so vociferous and extreme that the group kicked her out.

And in this series' case, those zombies were choking the streets of Ikebukuro.

The very city is being defiled.

To Youko, the animated series and live-action movie being shown to the nation was equivalent to dumping gasoline and toxic sludge all over Ikebukuro. The fact that there were residents who *welcomed* this horrible defilement was a sign that the world of harmony she sought was permanently shattered.

It should be noted that she did not know any of the finer points of the *Owl of the Peeping Dead* story.

She had neither watched the anime nor read the manga, and she hadn't seen the movie.

All she needed for her judgment was a simple synopsis and the promotional visuals that showed up when you searched for it online.

The setting: Ikebukuro overrun with zombies.

A movie poster with spilled blood as the center of its design.

These two things were all she needed to feel disgusted. She couldn't handle violent content being brought into a real city.

"How do you know what it's about if you haven't seen it?" people would ask her.

To them, Youko would confidently say, "I don't need to see it to know. The support from people like you, who would viciously attack my reputation, is the greatest possible proof that this franchise is utterly malicious and devoid of virtue."

Of course, people raided the message board and social media accounts of her website. Some people tried to argue in good faith and make her see sense, while others just piled on and left abusive, anonymous comments.

She picked up only the insults, published them on her site, and announced, "These disgusting people are the ones who support that awful, awful movie."

She ignored the good faith comments—not because she couldn't argue against them but because she pitied them. She thought, *They might seem calm, but the fact that they can rationally support this film is merely proof of how brainwashed they are. Nothing I can say to them will get through, the poor souls.*

The world that Youko envisioned was right and just, and anyone who believed in anything aside from that was either evil or a poor, pitiable victim of brainwashing.

Most frightening of all was that a number of people actually agreed with her and backed her up.

In most cases, they were people who signed on due to her outward concern of "preserving a pristine future for our children" and got steadily infected by her way of thinking. In a sense, perhaps her unwavering certainty gave her a kind of charisma to others.

In addition, the groups that sought stricter restrictions on content in movies, shows, manga, and video games found Youko's activism to be a convenient tool. They understood that she was an extremist, of course, but the furious and offensive reactions she elicited, which included death threats, were a useful thing to have as evidence.

When someone made a death threat toward Youko, they could publicize it greatly, influencing public opinion by telling the world, "This is what people who read violent, extreme manga do." Of course, if the rest of society knew how crazy Youko was, it would be less convincing, so they made certain to minimize Youko's profile as a victim.

As for her, Youko continued her activities all the while, heedless of the many different people taking advantage of the situation for their own reasons. With her sympathetic followers, she created the group People for the Calm Treatment of Ikebukuro, which she used to launch an all-out attack on *Owl of the Peeping Dead*.

It was a war that had lasted for years.

Despite her activities, the anime and movie were big hits, and the zombie story was a major part of pop culture around the city.

Last Halloween, the *OPD* production company and publisher started a promotion to get people dressed up as zombies to celebrate. The group came together to prevent this from happening and wound up getting arrested for interfering.

"But we were just trying to purify the evil vibes this horrible zombie-style event was creating," they protested, showing no understanding of where they had gone wrong. But they couldn't deny that the runaway freight train momentum of *OPD* was leaving them exhausted and dejected.

And that was when a miracle occurred.

To her, it was truly a message from the heavens.

Some person dressed as a character in *OPD* ambushed and attacked someone on the street.

Based on information they gleaned from the Net, they learned before the media did that the attacker was dressed up as the character known as the Dark Owl.

It's all over now.

We've won the war.

At last, the world will see and understand just how violent and evil and depraved these lost souls are.

The victims of the attacker were a sacrifice for the sake of harmony.

She and the rest of the group mourned the attack and its violence, and they rejoiced in it.

However, the media did not publicize the information about the Dark Owl. If anything, their reporting slowed to a trickle after the first day.

What could this mean?

Was *OPD* paying the media off to cover it up?

The group's hope quickly turned to despair.

Society did not seek harmony, they realized.

The unwelcome arrival of this truth drove Youko into a desperate frenzy. Her life's goal had been denied.

She destroyed all manner of things around her home, and tears of furious frustration blotted her pillow, many, many times...

And then she had an idea.

What if it just wasn't *enough*?

Did the noble goal of harmony require more hallowed sacrifices?

Upon this realization, she consulted with her trusted followers. These were not the influential people in the political groups that used her for their own purposes but the handful of people who truly believed in her ideals.

After a long period of persuasion, Youko and a number of her "agents of harmony" reached a conclusion.

In order to kill the devil, they had to sell their souls to it.

"We have to do this! We're sorry—we're so sorry!" they wailed as they bludgeoned their victims.

And with each groan of pain and each splash of blood, they could feel it happening.

They were surrounding themselves with an impurity that could never be wiped clean.

The Dark Owl was a shell of pure corruption around them. Even so, it was a step toward harmony in Ikebukuro.

They believed that when all of Ikebukuro was eventually purified that shell would break, and they would be reborn in a true sense—and so they continued to commit evil as the Dark Owl.

They would continue for as long as it took until people recognized the wickedness of the Dark Owl and the story that contained it.

Although they came to a realization one day: Someone else—probably the true, original attacker—had begun to hunt the city's unsavory scum.

"It's come at last...," she murmured.

Youko didn't know if this attacker was the same as the very first attacker, but she was absolutely certain that it was caused by the same wicked will of *OPD* that prevented their harmony from being realized.

By purging the city of its delinquents and creating a false sense of harmony, the other attacker was attempting to depict *OPD* as something harmless to society, even beneficial.

"More... We need to dedicate more sacrifices..."

There was only one way to fight back, to purify Ikebukuro: They had to shed more blood.

A fierce battle remained ahead of them, but there was no hesitation in Youko's eyes.

*   *   *

All their efforts were for the future of Ikebukuro. This was the ideal they held in their hearts as they searched for their latest sacrifice.

It was for Ikebukuro. To protect Ikebukuro from the hands of wicked pillagers.

Youko gripped the symbol of evil in her hand, the bandaged hammer.

It should also be noted that she was a resident of Saitama Prefecture; she did not live in Ikebukuro.

INTERMISSION
Online Rumors

On the Ikebukuro information site IkeNew! Version I.KEBU.KUR.O

New Post: Admin's predictions! Are there TWO attackers in Ikebukuro?!

Comment from IkeNew! *Administrator*

After examining the incidents of stweet viowence, I have come to a weawization.

I get the feewing that thewe isn't just one attackew.

By examining the map of where the attacks have happened, I've noticed there's a clear split in the spots where normal people are being attacked and where the bikers and street gang thugs are getting assauwwted.

Maybe the latter is the effect of some stweet confwict.

See, as long as you're dressed like the Dark Owl, anyone can be the stweet attackew.

Which means the decisive factor is whether the first couple to be attacked were normal people or wiving on the wougher side.

But I suppose how it started doesn't weawwy mattew.

The point is, at the current rate, the Dark Owl is gonna conquew da city.

*   *   *

But isn't it so mystewious?

The police should be able to investigate through the network of security camewas.

With all the attention on this, the fact that the attacks keep happening suggests that both sides responsible have some means of avoiding police suwveiwwance.

Or perhaps there's a different weason.

If there are really two sepawate attackews here, I await my many desewved compwiments.

Admin: Rira Tailtooth Zaiya

A selection of comments from the same site

- I knew that.

- What's up with that weird Snake Hands ad, Admin? *(Deleted minutes later)*

- Are you this late?! I knew that last week.

- What's your source for this info? They don't list attack locations or profiles of the victims in the newspaper.

- this is painful

- You want compliments? For being right about people being hurt?

- Admin's the attacker.

- God, shut up with this uwu shtick.

- The attacker is a hostess.

- Are any of these attacks even real? I think the media made it up.

- Hey, why do you delete every comment about Snake Hands? *(Deleted minutes later)*

- Snake Hands Snake Hands Snake Hands Snake Hands Snake Hands Snake Hands Snake Hands Snake Hands *(Deleted and user banned)*

♂♀

A selection of representative twits from the social network Twittia

So is the IkeNew admin just making stuff up now?

> → Nah, it's more like they're just ripping off the people freaking out on Twittia.

>> → Damn, that admin suuucks…

Isn't the Headless Rider involved with these attacks again?

> → I don't think it's right to blame everything on the Headless Rider.

>> → It's like they're so brain-dead, they don't realize that makes it harder to catch the real culprit.

>>> → You know you're responding to a meme, right?

In any case, the biggest victim here is *Owl of the Peeping Dead*, obviously.

> → Protect Ikebukuro! #DestroyOwlofthePeepingDead

> → Our children's future is being ruined. #DestroyOwlofthe PeepingDead

> → Save Ikebukuro from this evil artifice. #DestroyOwlofthe PeepingDead

>> → What the hell is this…?

>>> → If you write the full title instead of *OPD*, they use bots to reply to your twits. It's just the PC Bloodbags.

>>>> → I hear there's a couple dozen active PC Bloodbags.

>>>>> → Seriously? Don't they realize that only makes them look worse?

>>>>>> → Why would they? They can't tell reality from fantasy.

          *   *   *

So who's going down next time? Dragon Zombies?

→ Huh? Those guys are still around?

→ Their boss is back or something. They're riding all over.

→ God, I wish the attackers would hunt down all those bozos.

→ Especially after the Dollars disappeared.

→ Did they really?

→ What do you mean?

→ Maybe the Dollars or Yellow Scarves are behind this one, too?

→ The Dollars dissolved naturally.

→ Yeah, naturally. Meaning no one ever announced it was official.

→ And that would make it the perfect group to come back like zombies.

CHAPTER 4

CHAPTER 4
Keep Going, Leave It to Me

Ikebukuro, mixed commercial building—Holy Article Hall, 4F

There was an office building not terribly close to Ikebukuro Station. The first floor of the building, which did not have a wide footprint, was a business that dealt in imported Taiwanese goods. The second floor handled Taiwanese food, and the third, books. Each floor had a different kind of business in it, making for a lively atmosphere.

The fourth floor was an event space for the use of the businesses within the building. When nothing was happening, it often served as a hangout space for Dragon Zombie's leader, Libei Ying, a relative of the building's owner.

"So I wanted to ask, do you have any idea who might be doing these attacks?" Yahiro asked.

Libei shook his head with annoyance. "No… Are you saying you came here just to ask me that?"

"Yes."

"I'm surprised you knew where to find us."

"I asked Kuon," Yahiro explained simply, eliciting a smirk from Libei.

"Uh-huh. Kuon's that kid with the green hair, right? And how would he know that? Well, whatever."

At Libei's sides stood his two sisters. Elsewhere in the space lounged members of Dragon Zombies, watching Yahiro warily from a distance.

"I was hoping you might be coming to ask to join our little group. I guess that was too optimistic of me."

"I'm sorry."

"You don't need to apologize for that…but aren't you scared? Coming here to the hideout of a big, scary motorcycle gang?"

"I'm super scared," Yahiro admitted honestly. "But letting the attacker roam the streets is scarier, so…"

"Listen, maybe I shouldn't be saying this, but from my perspective, *you're* a lot scarier than this attacker. Right, Mr. Snake Hands?"

"Please don't. Why is everyone calling me by that nickname…?" Yahiro blushed slightly.

Of course, Libei himself was the one who spread that practice, but he showed no acknowledgment of that as he shook his head. "It's such a mysterious thing, isn't it? But don't worry—I think the nickname suits you."

"It does?"

"Why wouldn't it?"

"Well, that's good, I guess…," Yahiro mumbled.

Libei grinned. "Anyway, from our perspective, if you caught the attacker, that would help us out a ton. We're even willing to help you with this, you know."

"Thank you very much."

"Now, we've done some research on this case. To be honest, some people suspect us, which is why we're forced to take part in the whole exercise."

"Is that right?"

"Some stories say there are *two* attackers…and that one of them is our work. Either us or the Blue Squares."

Yahiro was aware of that theory. Kuon's sister was spreading that story on her websites that morning, but it also came up in conversation with Himeka and Aoba, so it didn't come as a surprise to him at this point.

"I don't think those rumors about the Blue Squares are true. They're on the hunt for the attacker, too."

"…Ah, yes. I believe you know someone who's in with them."

"In a manner of speaking, yes. I don't know them that well."

"Well, I'm not going to bother you about it, but I wouldn't go around announcing that, you understand? Just saying that you're friends with Blue Squares will make you a sworn enemy of Toramaru," Libei warned, smirking. "What a nasty bit of forced cooperation, though. I mean, it's still way better than teaming up with Jan-Jaka-Jan...but even so, we can't do anything together publicly. If any story starts up about Blue Squares and Dragon Zombies doing the same thing, it's gonna get everyone else's hackles up. They'll think we're forming an alliance."

"Is that how it works?"

"That *is* how it works," Libei said, his tone playful.

Yahiro felt like he'd had a similar vibe from a conversation partner earlier—with Aoba Kuronuma. "But you should be fine," he said, thinking carefully, "because I'm not here asking you to do anything—I just wanted to talk."

"Oh, really? Maybe that's what *you* think, but the kids you're in with might want to use us, wouldn't they?" Libei drawled ironically.

"Hmm...I don't really know how all that stuff works," Yahiro said. Then he thought about Kuon, his client. "Oh, but at the very least, he's *definitely* using me. He said so."

"Sounds like a bad boss." Libei smirked.

"But it's fine. I don't mind," Yahiro reassured him.

"Huh? Does that really make it better?" Libei stared at Yahiro for a while, then sighed and continued, "Anyway...if you don't care, then I guess that's that. In any case, neither Dragon Zombies nor the Blue Squares can make a big show about this. So there's no using numbers to try to overpower the attacker or gang up on them like last time, got it? Then again, I guess you solved that one on your own, huh."

Libei thought about that one a bit more, then adopted a rather wicked grin and jabbed a finger right at Yahiro. "So I'm thinking...if another mysterious phantom like Snake Hands takes out the attacker, no one will have to suspect us or the Blue Squares of having any part of it. What do you think?"

"..." Yahiro took some time to consider this, and then he nodded. "Yes, that does make sense."

"Wow, he actually bought it."

"Well...it does make sense. If a mystery phantom catches the attacker, nobody else gets blamed...and if the attacker has friends, you're safe from them...," Yahiro murmured to himself. Then his face lit up, and he bowed. "Thank you very much, Mr. Libei! I think I figured it out!"

A few minutes later, Yahiro was on his way out, having finished the conversation.

Libei watched him go, and when the boy was out of sight, his smile vanished.

"He's in trouble," he said to no one but himself, his concern genuine but also wary.

"He really needs a friend who can slam on his brakes for him—good or bad."

♂♀

Kotonami apartment

When Kuon returned home, he made dinner like always and left a portion outside his sister's room, then went into his own and turned on the computer.

He organized the information he found on the screen and considered what was to come.

"Hmm...I think the moment is right," he said to himself, lifting his arms to stretch with a little smile playing across his lips.

At that moment, his phone vibrated.

"Hello?"

"Heya, Kuon. How are ya?"

"Hi, Sis. I put your food outside the door. Eat up before it gets cold."

"Yeah, no worries. But before that, I wanted to tell you something."

It was an everyday event for the two of them to speak on the phone from adjacent rooms. It wasn't because they were particularly distant. Kuon understood that this was the best way to close the distance with Nozomi.

"What's that?"

"You gonna wrap it all up over the holiday? The street attacker thing."

"I suppose. It'll be real annoying to do once school starts again… and Yahiro apparently went to the Dragon Zombies looking for info. If I let him wander off on his own any further, it's going to get out of hand," he said, sounding fatigued.

"You're worried for him," Nozomi teased.

"Am not."

"I get it. He's your very first friend."

"No, he's not! I've had friends before!" he snarled, gritting his teeth.

Through the speaker, his sister teased, "Just so you know, Kuronuma and his gang don't count as friends."

"Huh? They don't?"

"Not if neither side trusts the other."

"…I don't think someone you trust in every regard is a friend, either," said Kuon, sighing.

"Really?" She chuckled. "At the very least, Yahiro seems to think of you as a friend."

"That's not my problem. He's just that naive." After a moment's pause, he told his sister, "After all, I'm forcing him to do all the dirty work on this one."

He smiled wickedly.

On the inside, he remembered his encounter with a researcher one year ago.

♂♀

One year ago—Ikebukuro

The moment he mentioned the name Izaya Orihara, a woman said with scorn, "You want to know about that idiot?"

"I've heard that you know more about him than anyone else does," Kuon said.

The long-haired woman clicked her tongue. "And this is what I get for coming back to Japan on work. Well, I don't know if he's alive or dead, but either way, he's got a skill for annoying me."

And with that, the woman who once served as Izaya's assistant, Namie Yagiri, began to talk about her former employer.

"How was he able to control the things that happened around town? Well, that's where you're confused," she began.

"Huh?"

"In nearly all cases, he wasn't actually controlling anything. He was just unleashing sparks. And he enjoyed the result, whether they started fires or went out right away. Whatever happened, he just gloated and acted like that was the 'right' answer, so from a distance, it just looked like he was manipulating things to his benefit."

"But I don't think that's all it was. I mean, there are people whose lives were ruined because he was pulling strings...," Kuon insisted, dark flames burning in his eyes.

At the time, he still looked like a model student; he hadn't yet dyed his hair green. Namie seemed to take an interest in him after seeing the burning look in his eyes, and her attitude softened.

"...Oh? So you're not here to praise Izaya? You hate him?"

"Uh, I didn't say that..."

"I like you. So I'll tell you for free that he did indeed have total control over a few incidents. And a few people's minds, I think. But there was a reason behind that. It's the primary reason he was so crazy and not easily mimicked. Something that no sane person would ever try."

Namie sounded like she was reminiscing fondly on the past.

"When he really, truly wanted to control everything, he always placed himself in the most dangerous position. Whatever event was happening, he made sure he was in the deepest, darkest spot. Wherever his life would be the most immediately in danger, he performed the dirtiest task."

"..."

"In fact, it was when he did anything from a perfectly safe position that the results were the worst. I guess it's the difference in the amount he was willing to sacrifice. They say things like, 'Only those who are willing to be killed have the right to kill,' but in Izaya's case, it was more like he was willing to be killed to have the right to slap someone on the cheek."

She looked Kuon in the eyes, seemingly staring right into his mind.

"If you want to be like him, it will come down to whether or not you're willing to risk that."

" . . . "

Intimidated, Kuon managed to stare back without looking away. Namie sighed.

"Well, to be honest, whether or not you get stuck in the swamp and drown is none of my concern. If you get involved with him—whatever form that takes—you need to be on your guard, or you'll get sucked in and spiral into your own downfall."

"So why didn't you get sucked into Izaya's whirlpool? How come you didn't get brainwashed when you were so close to him?" he asked.

Namie stared into the distance. A blissful look came over her face.

"There is a support at the center of my being that keeps me sane at all times. I wouldn't let someone like him drag me under."

♂♀

That's right.

I've got my own support keeping me sane.

The recollection of his conversation with Namie gave Kuon the resolve to make a decision.

"Sis."

"What?"

"I love you."

"I know."

As family? As man and woman? Neither one knew.

But Kuon said it anyway and added, "I hate humanity. I love only you."

"Are you saying this to yourself?"

"Yeah. Sorry, Sis. Just let me have this one."

"I don't mind. We're brother and sister," she said, cackling with laughter. It brought a smile to Kuon's face.

Shortly after their call ended, Kuon clutched the phone.

Then he rested his forehead against the wall to his sister's room and muttered softly to himself.

"I can be as evil as I need to be. I'll do the things Izaya Orihara couldn't do. I'll use my friends and send them to hell."

The look on his face was just a bit mournful as he added one last comment.

"...And if I make life harder on you, Sis, I'm sorry."

♂♀

Ikebukuro—final day of the holiday week

One of the street attackers, Shouya Ajimura, walked the evening streets with a pensive look on his face.

"That was a close one yesterday... Didn't think I was going to actually *miss* on that swing..."

He'd been aiming to knock out his target in one blow, but the man with the dreads managed to dodge his swing. Then he lost his balance and got hurt anyway, but it was a far cry from the punishment Ajimura intended to inflict.

"Dammit... Stupid thug..."

It was the man who always hung around with Shizuo Heiwajima.

Even Ajimura was aware of Shizuo Heiwajima's superhuman strength. Which is why he chose to attack someone close to him, in order to deliver a mental blow to Ikebukuro's symbol of violence instead.

But the attack missed at the last second, and in the chaos that followed, he very nearly got destroyed.

They might be scum, but it's scary dealing with men who fight all the time. I didn't expect that Horada guy to fight back the other day, either. Dammit! Dammit!

"..."

Ajimura paused in that line of thinking and reconsidered his actions.

He lacked the self-awareness to realize he was the street attacker, but he had utter faith in his actions regardless. There was just one thing that Ajimura wondered about. When he swung his hammer of justice down upon Horada, there was one thing that felt wrong.

After the first counterattack, when he got punched in return—for some reason, that Horada man was already bleeding from the head and was on the ground by the time Ajimura got back up.

So who did that?

He was acting alone.

He told the people on his site, "That wasn't a street attack—it was an act of justice," but he still hadn't told them that it was *his* handiwork.

It was too early to reveal that yet.

Still too early.

Only after the unfairly poor reputation of the so-called random street attacks had been swept clean could he tell the world that he was the Dark Owl. Only then would he and *OPD* truly be one. The world would take on its true and proper form.

With that inner monologue complete, he reached the answer to his suspicions.

What if that was actually the work of a fan of OPD...a fan of me?

Perhaps it was a like-minded fellow, a sympathetic comrade, who laid Horada out on the ground.

He'd chosen Horada because he was a famous ruffian in the area, according to the stories the folks on his site repeated.

Or maybe it was just someone who had a pure, personal grudge against Horada.

But whether coincidence or fate, someone had come out of the shadows to help.

What could that be if not evidence that the world had *chosen* him for its noble quest?

Ajimura's head bobbed with great determination.

He was doing this for *OPD*.

Even if he wound up arrested, the police wouldn't charge him with much.

After all, he was merely doing what the police *should have* been doing all along.

He chuckled to himself as he packed up his Boston bag.

He simply laughed.

Man, this is fun.

This really is my true life at last.

Only by dipping into the thrill of attacking people on the street did he feel alive, for the first time in his life.

And to keep that feeling going, he headed out once again—the weight of the wrapped-up hammer hidden in the second compartment of the bag pressing against the palm of his hand.

♂♀

Evening—outside Yahiro's apartment

Yahiro returned to his apartment building as the sun was going down.

"Yo. Seems like you had a good day out on the town again," said Saburo Togusa, who had been humming as he washed his van, upon seeing Yahiro's arrival.

"Yes, I did a lot of traveling around."

"Where'd you go?"

"Ummm…to the Holy Article Hall and stuff like that…" Yahiro didn't really feel a necessity to hide where he'd been.

"Ah, the one with the Taiwanese restaurant? Dragon Zombie likes to hang out there, so be careful you don't get dragged into a fight, hear?"

"Uh, right," said Yahiro vaguely, sensing that he probably shouldn't mention who he was meeting there.

"Hmm… They say people are getting attacked on the street, so watch out for that, too."

"Thank you, I will." Yahiro soon realized that he'd never actually asked Saburo what he knew about the street attacker. "There was someone attacking people on the street before, wasn't there?"

"Hmm? Oh…you mean the slasher?" Togusa's eyes narrowed just a bit. Yahiro did not miss it.

It wasn't the disturbed look of someone talking about violence but a look of deep, emotional connection.

Huh? Does Saburo…know something about the slasher?

He was considering how he might ask further about this, but it was at that very moment that his phone buzzed with an incoming call.

"Hello, this is Mizuchi speaking."

"Oh, heya! This is Karisawa. You doing anything tonight, Yappy?"

"Ah, good evening," he said, realizing that Yappy was probably supposed to be her nickname for him. But he couldn't be sure, so he offered a hesitant "Er, I suppose so?"

"Oh, really? Well, the holiday week is over, so why don't we meet up to compare notes?"

"...Okay, that sounds like a good idea." Yahiro figured it would be good to hear what others had learned, too. If the attacks kept happening, it really was going to have an effect on *OPD* sooner or later.

"All right, cool. Well, I'd like to introduce you to some folks, so could you make it to Tokyu Hands soon? Kuocchi's got something keeping him from making it today. What about you?"

"Yes, no problem. Well, I'll see you there."

Yahiro ended the call, then spun right around on his heel.

"Sorry, Saburo, I've got to head out again."

"Damn, being a student is busy work, huh? Just watch out for the—," Togusa started to say, until *he* was interrupted by his phone. He put it to his ear and said, "Oops, sorry about that... Who, them?"

Yahiro didn't want to interrupt his conversation, so he simply bowed and made to leave, except that Togusa said, "Okay, got it. I'll head right over... Oh, hang on, Yahiro!"

He ended the call and stopped the younger boy.

"Are you heading toward Ikebukuro Station?"

"Uh, yes. To Sixtieth Floor Street."

"Cool! Perfect timing."

"?"

To Yahiro's surprise, Saburo opened the door of his van.

"A friend just called me over there, too. Hop in, and I'll give you a ride."

Shinra's apartment, evening

As the six o'clock news played in the background, Celty offered Shinra a comment.

"I know I'm not exactly finding the attacker, either, but you'd really expect the police to nab this guy by now."

For one thing, it would take a huge load off her shoulders if the police caught them first. She wouldn't be able to fulfill the request from Yumasaki and Karisawa, but they couldn't complain too much if the cops caught the bad guy. The same was probably true for Shizuo.

There was still the faint chance that Shizuo might storm the jail and pound the culprit into dust, but he seemed to feel that he owed the police something, so she thought it was unlikely he'd do anything that drastic.

Which meant that the most peaceful solution of all was for the police to make a clean arrest of the street attacker. That was her hope, at least.

But Shinra only said, "Uh, sure. It'll probably take a bit longer, though."

"Why? They just have to track down whoever's bought those pajamas, right? And aren't they in a better position to do that than anyone else?"

"...Well, that's the thing about those *kigurumi* pajamas."

"What about them?" she asked, not seeing his point.

Shinra exhaled deeply. "They're a big trend around Ikebukuro. I bet several hundred people have bought a set."

"...Huh?"

"They sold the pajamas as fan merch, but when the first rumors of the incident started online, people bought a ton of them, fearing they'd all get taken down. And when some stores doing retail honored the request to stop selling, others with a huge stock started selling them online instead. Ha-ha-ha."

"Wha-wha-wha...?"

She nearly fell to her knees, but Shinra wasn't done yet.

"On top of that, there are people online involved in some very unsavory games, knowing that you'll really stand out by wearing them now. So when the police think they've found the attacker, it turns out to just be some teenagers wearing the outfit. It's happened several times already."

"If they're messing around like that, they should just be arre—"

Only calm reason stopped Celty from finishing that sentence. *I really shouldn't be saying that and tempting fate,* she thought, envisioning the traffic cop who always chased her, and she shivered.

She revised. *"...I can't believe they don't have anything better to do..."*

"Yeah. Apparently, there's a bunch of online trolls who called themselves Underars."

"Underars?" Celty repeated. It sounded oddly familiar.

"Yep. So the Dollars are gone, right? These are the kids who can't seem to accept that yet, so they made a new anonymous online group to replace them. They throw tags on the street and call it guerrilla art; they scatter daikon radish seeds in empty lots around the city; they do all kinds of stuff."

"People do that?"

"I'm guessing it's a combination of *Under,* like 'underground,' and *Dollars.* Under-ars. Unde-rars. What's *rars*?"

"Plan."

"Huh?" Shinra said, baffled by Celty's response.

"There's a word that sounds similar in Icelandic, ráð. It means 'plan' or 'advice.' Things like that."

"Wow, I had no idea! You're so smart, Celty! You even know Scandinavian words!"

"Yeah, someone I knew from waaaay back had a nickname that started with the same sound...but that's neither here nor there. The issue at hand is the attacker," she said, abruptly changing the topic and making a sighing gesture. *"So the clothes have an excuse. But there's no excuse for the hammer, right?"*

"Well, true. But there are ways to hide that, right? Attach something hard and heavy to the end of a stick and wrap it up with a bandage. You could make one with a pestle and a rock, as easy as that."

"...So it seems harder to search for than I thought..."

"Now, if they catch the guy in the act, it's a no-brainer. I could be bait, Celty," Shinra suggested. She jabbed his forehead with a finger.

"Well, how are you going to lure the attacker? And you're not allowed to do something that dangerous, even if it works."

"Even though you do dangerous things, Celty? You're so selfish."

"That's right. I'm being selfish. Is that not allowed?"

"Of course it's allowed. But I might just be selfish in return," he said with an impish grin. Then he smacked his fist into his palm. "That's it! It'll take time, but I know how to ensure we find the attacker!"

"Really?"

"Yep. First, I'll use Saika on every person in Ikebukuro, then..."

"Never mind," she said, not bothering to listen to the rest.

She was just going back to the drawing board when her notification alert went off.

"Speak of the devil, there's my employer."
"Yumasaki?"
"That's my client. My employer, as I mentioned earlier...is that Kotonami boy," Celty explained, opening the message.

The text was brief and simple.

"I will capture the attacker tonight. Please come to my apartment building."

♂♀

Ikebukuro—night

Youko Shirobishi was panicked.

Everything was supposed to go well. This was supposed to be the perfect target. How did it come to this?

The young man's voice cut through her confusion.

"Heh-heh-heh, I never expected to be made a target... I guess I really am the chosen hero, guided by two-dimensional fate and destiny! It won't be long until I get into a car accident and end up reincarnated into another world!"

Standing before her was a narrow-eyed young man holding a *fire-spewing fire extinguisher.*

Youko thought as hard as she could, while the man prattled on about nonsense she didn't understand.

How had she gotten into this predicament?

♂♀

Ten minutes earlier

Youko was walking around Ikebukuro, searching for the day's sacrifice, when she found the thing she hated most at the moment.

Owl of the Peeping Dead.

The wicked cause of all this evil continued to fill the city with its malevolent energy.

While it wasn't quite the smash hit it was at the start of the street attacks, the return of the live-action movie to theaters was a sign of its popularity, and there were still posters around the neighborhood.

How can anyone be smiling while this is going on? she thought with outrage. The world was so unfair. She had to be the one to correct it.

She continued on her way, glaring at her surroundings, seeking a sacrifice.

On the final night of the holiday week, with the workday coming up in the morning, there was considerably less foot traffic than there had been the night before.

Prior to now, she hadn't chosen any particular targets—simply those who were easiest to attack.

Could that have been a mistake, however?

Maybe she ought to be acting with a firm, clear purpose.

With that idea in mind, she murmured to herself, "Yes, that's right… That's true… It's why that pharisee got ahead of me," referring to her label for the other false attacker.

Hatred shone in her eyes, hatred toward a singular target in the scene around her.

A van parked in a lot.

A van with a picture from some manga plastered on its door.

Ugh, it makes me feel sick. Manga on the side of your car.

Her hatred for *OPD* had developed into a hatred of all things anime, and she stared at the group surrounding the van with utter loathing. One of them, a young man with narrow eyes holding an *OPD* fan, was in a state of agitation.

Look, there's one of the scum now!

She walked closer, until she could hear what the young man was insisting on.

"My point is—! We need to get the word out that *OPD* isn't at fault for any of this! The street attacker's just an *OPD* hater! A hater trying to ruin *OPD*'s spotless reputation!"

Youko abruptly felt as though someone had knocked the wind out of her. The man's accusation was accurate, and it made her worry they knew who she was.

Next, her head swooned. It was impossible for her to fathom that there were still people under the mistaken belief that *OPD* was innocent.

How can there be such an idiot in Ikebukuro?

The question of whether *OPD* was guilty or innocent had been settled long ago. Youko had delivered her verdict and found it guilty.

How could *Owl of the Peeping Dead* possibly be more malicious? Its very existence had forced her into the act of attacking people on the street.

If the thing that turned me into a violent attacker isn't evil, then what is?!

There might not have been a single, objectively logical thought left in her mind. Nevertheless, her brain worked as a system guiding her toward one goal.

She made her choice.

She chose today's sacrifice—the street attacker's victim.

And then her logic completed its loop. This was not punishment but salvation.

He had eyes for nothing but this evil malignancy, but her blow would awaken him. And then the foolish, wicked believers would finally learn their lesson. They would see what a tragic end awaited them by the example of their fellow. And then they would be saved. They would be redeemed.

At least in her mind.

She was already contradicting her train of thought from just a few seconds earlier, but she would not be dissuaded from her goal.

Youko set her sights on the narrow-eyed man.

She waited at a distance; her timing was good because their group was just splitting up, and within a few minutes, the man left them and headed toward the busier part of town.

Ah, yes. Everything is working to make my quest easier.

This is solid proof that I am doing the right thing.

I should have been carefully choosing my sacrifices!

The only thing she shared in common with the other street attacker was a belief that the world itself was on her side.

She watched the man go and waited for her opportunity to arrive. Once he was in a reasonably secluded area, she began her preparations.

The man received a call at that point, and he pulled his phone out and proceeded to hold a conversation.

Youko considered this her chance.

She took off her outerwear, immediately producing a different kind of fabric from underneath.

Within just a few seconds, she was dressed in the Dark Owl costume she wore under her regular clothes, and she snuck up on the man from behind.

She started slow.

Then she got faster.

Holding her breath to make as little noise as possible, she pulled out the bandaged hammer hidden under her outfit, then raised it high overhead.

But in the next moment…

"Look out!"

A distant shout drew the narrow-eyed man's attention toward his rear.

"What?" he said, holding the phone, face slack—and that was when he met eyes with Youko, standing behind him, hammer raised.

They both stared.

"…"

"…"

"Die!" Youko snarled, after briefly drawing a blank. She swung down the hammer.

"Whaaa—?!" the man yelped, dodging just in the nick of time and landing on his bottom in the street.

I can get him!

She glanced behind her and saw two figures running toward her, but they were still too far away. She had plenty of time to hit the man and escape.

In fact, at this point she didn't even *need* to get away.

The most important thing of all was to turn this owl-worshipping scum into a human sacrifice.

If she got caught, the police, courts, and society itself would be understanding.

They would realize that the wicked owl caused her to do this.

And that would lead to the necessary restrictions even faster.

She had to create this final sacrifice in order to bring it all about. She earnestly believed this was necessary for a healthy future for Ikebukuro. That was why she did not hesitate to swing her hammer down at the man sitting on the asphalt.

There was no point or need to worry about a nonfatal blow. All that mattered was to make sure her swing left the man unmoving.

However...

Gank! Something loudly struck the hammer in her hand.

"?!"

She looked at her target with shock and saw that the narrow-eyed man had instantly removed his backpack and held it up as a shield against her hammer.

Still, something felt off about the impact it made. That unnerved and confused her.

It was as though his backpack was full of metal of some kind.

And in the next moment, her confusion thawed, and a new question arose in her mind.

"The attacker...," murmured the narrow-eyed man as he pulled something out of the backpack.

...A...fire...extinguisher...?

It was so out of place for the situation that she wasn't sure what to think.

Until the very next moment when flames poured out of the fire extinguisher.

♂♀

Just minutes before, the boy who later shouted the warning was seated in the back of Togusa's van.

"Man...I can't believe you know them." Saburo Togusa sighed from the driver's seat. He'd driven to the meeting spot to drop Yahiro off, but the boy actually greeted Karisawa and Yumasaki first, which was Togusa's first inkling that they'd all met already.

"What?! Why is Yahiro getting out of Togucchi's van?! Is that a magic trick?!" Karisawa exclaimed.

"It might be sorcery...or some kind of psychic recognition-manipulation power!" Yumasaki said.

"Huh? You guys know Saburo?" Yahiro asked.

"Know him? We were planning to introduce you to him today!"

"Oh, I see. Well, I'm actually staying at the Togusas' apartment building..."

"Whoa, whoa, whoa! Wait just a minute! What's up with you guys?!"

Once the dust had settled and everyone had a chance to explain themselves, Togusa finally accepted the situation. The group concluded brief introductions, and then Yumasaki and Karisawa kicked out the vehicle's driver so they could hold a "secret discussion" inside, using the van as a meeting room.

Togusa was chagrined, but he said it "always happened this way" and stepped outside with the last member of the group.

Well, if he's doing something with those two, it's gotta be something otaku related. In fact, he low-key looks like a kid who reads a lot of manga. Maybe he's doing doujinshi or cosplay or somethin'. Still...poor kid, catching their attention.

Togusa felt conflicted about this development, knowing how dangerous the pair of them could be in the right circumstances. On the other hand, when they were just indulging their hobbies, they were well-behaved, and the pair were experts in their field.

It's not like I can tell him not to hang out with them. But if something should go wrong...what would I tell the family...?

He walked around, thinking hard, and returned a while later to see that they had left the van after finishing their secret business.

Karisawa was stopping by Tokyu Hands before going home, so Yumasaki headed off on his own.

Well, there are plenty of folks making doujinshi who don't tell their families about it, I hear. Guess I don't need to bother him by asking about it.

As he left the parking garage, Saburo spoke over his shoulder to Yahiro. "Listen, I don't know what you're doing with those guys, and I'm not gonna pry...but choose your friends wisely, okay?"

"Thanks. This helped me realize that they're safe and cool. I'm not a good judge of character, but when I learned you were friends with them, that settled it for me."

"Uh...well...," Togusa stammered, no idea what to say.

The guy in the passenger seat laughed. "Ha! He's got you there, Togusa."

"Yeah, I know, but..."

The other guy, who wore a bandanna around his head, was someone Yumasaki and Karisawa had already introduced to Yahiro. But because they took Yahiro out right afterward, he'd hardly spoken a word to the man.

Kadota sensed that Yahiro was feeling awkward around him, so he turned back and said, "Let me introduce myself again. I'm Kadota. I've known this guy for years now. And I've been to your apartment building a couple times."

"Oh, I see. I'm Yahiro Mizuchi. It's nice to meet you."

"Mizuchi's a strange name. Where are you from?"

"Akita Prefecture."

"Wow. That's pretty far away from here."

Saburo chuckled and told him, "Get this. Right after he came here to Ikebukuro, he went out and got beat up by Shizuo."

"What? Are you serious?"

"Yes," Yahiro admitted.

Kadota's eyes bulged. "Why would you piss him off?"

"Well...it was my fault. My friend from class coincidentally happened to make him mad... I tried to stop him, and then it turned into a fight."

"Ah, so that's how it happened."

Kadota still found it curious that Yahiro described it as a fight, but he offered advice as a resident of Ikebukuro regardless.

"Listen, he'll get pissed real quick, but he's not unreasonable. As long as you apologize, he'll forgive you."

"That's what Saburo told me. I want to give him a proper apology the next time we meet."

"That's a good idea."

Saburo grimaced and explained, "The thing is, he got beat up by Shizuo, got right to his feet, and walked home, then went to school like normal the next day. That's pretty impressive, don't you think?"

"Damn...that *is* impressive." Kadota stared at him in amazement.

Yahiro played it down. "No, it was just luck. I didn't get hit in dangerous spots, I guess you'd say..."

It was certainly the honest truth from *his* perspective, but Kadota was utterly confused; he wasn't able to imagine this timid-looking boy having the hardy muscles needed to withstand that kind of punishment.

"I dunno, though," he murmured. "Then again, they say Shizuo's mellowed out a lot lately..."

Kadota was planning to drop the subject and talk about more mundane topics, when he noticed that Yahiro was turning his head, looking intently out the window.

"What's up? Did you forget something?"

"No..." Yahiro paused for a few moments, looked around a little more, then asked, "Um, which direction is Yumasaki's house?"

"Huh? He's right in the middle of the residential area north of here... Why?"

"Is that a pretty busy area?"

"Well, it's residential, so at this hour...probably not?"

It was already after ten o'clock. If you weren't in the busy commercial areas, that was an hour of day when people were already home.

"Do you mind letting me off here? And tell me the way to get to his house."

"Huh? Hey, what's up? You've got school tomorrow, right? Don't stay out all night," Saburo warned, out of concern for his tenant's school performance.

But with some consternation, shouting quickly as though he had no time, Yahiro replied, "I hope I'm just mistaken about this...but I think someone's after Yumasaki and Karisawa."

"Huh?" repeated Saburo, but Yahiro was already taking something dark out of his bag.

He bowed and said gravely, "Please just let me out. I'll explain later. And if you could, call Yumasaki and tell him to keep an eye out... I just realized I only exchanged numbers with Karisawa."

"Okay, but—," Togusa stammered, but Kadota saw the look in Yahiro's eyes and cut him off.

"Stop at the corner up there."

"Come on—are you serious?"

"I know where he lives. It's quicker to run from this point than turn the car around," Kadota insisted, removing his seat belt so he could join Yahiro.

"I'll show you the way. Follow me."

♂♀

That was what led to the present moment.

Youko batted at her clothes in a panic; she could sense that parts of them were burning.

Then she gripped her hammer again, feeling a cold sweat break out over her face beneath the hood that hid it.

What is this?

What's going on?!

Meanwhile, Yumasaki's palms were also slick.

He really didn't think he'd *actually* become the street attacker's target.

He'd modified a fire extinguisher into a homemade flamethrower and had been carrying it around ever since Kadota got hit by that car and the group had gone searching for the culprit.

For the last few days, he'd been fantasizing about being targeted by the attacker, so when he walked the streets alone, he always had a counterattacking plan at the forefront of his mind.

It was basically no different from being a student and thinking, *If a terrorist came into this classroom right now, this is the coolest way I could possibly fight them off!*

There was never any terrorist attack on his school—but here and now, that fantasy had been realized.

If a normal human being was faced with an actual terrorist or random street attacker, they wouldn't be able to react according to the fantasy. They'd freeze up in a panic.

But Yumasaki was not exactly a normal person. That was the only difference.

On the one hand, you had the famous street attacker, carrying a hammer.

On the other hand, a young man carrying a modified flame-throwing fire extinguisher, muttering bizarre statements to himself.

Normally they would *both* need to be arrested, but that did not matter to Yumasaki. If he could stop the attacker's spree of violence, it would be worth the arrest for excessive self-defense. As he pulled the lever on the weapon, he reminded himself that when he got arrested, he should claim he was definitely *not* a fan of *OPD* and that he enjoyed getting his sick thrills from watching disaster clips on the news and *not* from manga.

Flame burst from the nozzle.

The attacker's limbs flopped and flailed as they backed away.

"Now behave yourself! It's time to face the music!"

"What…what is this? It's not fair!" said a woman's voice, which was momentarily surprising to Yumasaki, but it did not stop him from pointing the extinguisher's nozzle at her.

"Not fair? How rude! Who decided that you couldn't use a flamethrower with the Brawling skill?!" he bellowed.

The attacker shrieked hysterically, "I don't understand what you're saying, you sick freak!"

"Says the person attacking people on the street! Get arrested and face justice, and then you'll look like the zombies you've disgraced! We'll see how you like it then!"

"What are you going to do to me, you sick freak?!"

"I'll be the one asking the questions…and I'll take my sweet time doing it!"

While they bantered back and forth, Yumasaki spotted people running in their direction.

They were too far away to make out by sight, but from their outfits, he recognized Yahiro and Kadota.

Yahiro was closer than Kadota, so Yumasaki shouted, "Yahi… Ah, watch out, it's dangerous!"

He very nearly let Yahiro's name slip in the presence of the street attacker but had the quick thinking to switch to something else. He'd heard about Yahiro's reputation, but he couldn't tell a high schooler to help him fight the violent attacker—plus, he could handle this one by himself.

So Yumasaki's initial plan was to get her to drop her weapon, then have Kadota tie her up—except that he was caught off guard by what the approaching boy yelled back.

"Look out! *Behind you!*"

"Huh?"

Yumasaki recognized extreme consternation in the boy's voice, so he turned quickly, while keeping the nozzle of the extinguisher pointed at the attacker.

And there stood a figure dressed in the *kigurumi* pajama outfit of the Dark Owl—raising a bandaged hammer in preparation to swing it at Yumasaki.

♂♀

That moment—Ikebukuro

Shouya Ajimura leisurely followed his target: a delinquent youth walking down a secluded street without a care in the world.

Walking the streets at night when the street attacker is out on the prowl? These delinquents are so stupid. Ajimura chuckled to himself as he approached.

He had a very clear reason for choosing this boy as a target.

It was because they bumped into each other in town, and the boy said to Ajimura, "Ow. Don't rub your stank-ass sweat on me."

Despite the fact that the other guy had bumped into Ajimura, he had complained and insulted him in an arrogant manner. The boy was so much younger, he might have been an entire rotation of the Chinese zodiac behind Ajimura. He found it annoying but also gratifying.

Could it have been a gift from God?

Or was the city itself bringing him a sacrifice?

It was hard to believe his luck, being greeted by a remorseless target for justice so directly and without hesitation.

Ordinarily, he would have preferred to go after a more infamous delinquent, but it was best not to push his luck now. He'd just failed in his attack on Shizuo Heiwajima's friend, after all.

So Ajimura very carefully trailed the boy, until the area around them looked more and more like an ideal place for him to conduct his violent "fan activities."

They were far from the shopping district now. When the youth began to loiter alone in a nearby park, Ajimura stealthily slipped into the shadows.

Apartment building fences left open. Narrow back alleys. Piles of materials left stacked at random.

It would be nearly impossible to change outfits in the commercial area near the train station, but here in these secluded streets, it was a different story.

Ajimura had put on the pajama onesie before leaving home. But he had the hood pulled back and hidden inside his jacket, leaving only the black bottoms of the *kigurumi* visible.

The bottoms were made of completely black material, so it was hard to distinguish them from ordinary tracksuit pants or sweats. In a darkened street at night, that kind of distinction was impossible to make.

It took only a second for Ajimura to remove the jacket, completing his outfit. Then he slipped the jacket inside of his onesie, making his stomach look bulged. Thus, by pulling his hood over his head, he turned into the Dark Owl just seconds after slipping into the shadows.

Once he was certain there was no one else around, he approached the delinquent from behind, undetected.

Just like always.

There was no reason to hesitate.

He had to make up for his failure to hit Shizuo Heiwajima's friend. He squeezed the hammer, feeling its reassuring sturdiness in his palm.

This is it. This is the sensation. The elation that grips my entire being. Like I'm not myself.

But that's wrong. This is the real me, the Dark Owl. I am the real Dark Owl.

Step by step, he snuck closer.

That's right, I have a companion.

He looked at the figure of the Dark Owl, standing next to the delinquent, and nodded firmly.

A companion who will help…me…

The Dark Owl was looking back at him.

Me? ...Me—me—me—me—me??????????

There was a Dark Owl there, a Dark Owl who was not him.

Ajimura was baffled.

Wh-who, who, who?

The real thing! Is that...the real...street attacker?!

Or are they a c-collaborator? A helper of mine? Which, wh-wh-wh-which?

Even in his mind, he couldn't keep himself from stammering. Sweat suddenly flooded from all his pores, making the inside of his suit a clammy mess.

And while he stood rooted to the spot with mental shock, the other Dark Owl lifted their hammer high...

And swung it down on the delinquent youth.

After the briefest of pauses, the boy crumpled to the ground in the middle of the park.

That was when Ajimura understood.

Standing there across from him was a fellow agent of justice.

The world was being born anew—for his sake.

♂♀

Ikebukuro Station—east gate exit

"You sure about this, Mr. Horada? Didn't they say you'd be hospitalized through next week?"

"Don't play games with my natural healing ability, shithead," Horada snarled. Bandages were wrapped all around his body, and he walked with a very distinct and awkward limp. Around him, his younger companions shared worried, uncertain looks.

He wasn't in any state to be walking around, but if he stayed at the hospital, Izumii was likely to show up again, so he practically threatened the doctor into letting him leave.

Belatedly, he realized that might tip off the police, but dealing with them would still be better than waiting where Izumii could sneak into his room at night and break his bones with a hammer.

So Horada decided to leave and dragged his followers with him around Ikebukuro, in search of the street attacker in person.

"But, Mr. Horada, you don't think we'll find the attacker hanging out right outside the station, do you?"

"How the hell should I know? Some folks got hit by the slasher right near the station, don't ya remember?"

"Well, yeah, that's true. But while a lot of the street attacks happened around Ikebukuro, they're also happening in Shinjuku and Setagaya and stuff. I don't think sticking to this one area is gonna turn up anything," complained a companion who'd spent half a day walking around with him.

Ugh...these idiots... I feel like they're not takin' me as seriously since Shizuo whupped my ass...

The terror of nearly dying in that attack flooded back into his mind. It even made the bruises he got from the street attacker throb. But the youngsters had no idea what kind of hell (of his own making) he'd been through, and they remained skeptical.

"Is it really true there were over five attackers?"

"What? What are you saying? You think I was bullshitting about that? Huh?!" he snarled, menacing the younger guy. But because of his wounds, his movement was unsteady and unimpressive, undercutting the intended effect.

"No, I'm just saying, if there are that many of them, they'll stand out. If they were changing into the outfit off to the side, there couldn't be more than one or two..."

The younger guy stopped there, staring at the crowd around them with a slack look on his face.

"Hmm? Hey, what's up?" Horada asked him, then looked in the same direction.

There was *black* there.

It was right outside the station.

In the midst of the bright lights, a black figure stood still.

And the moment he saw it, Horada's face paled.

"Wha...ah...kah..."

The Dark Owl.

The attacker who smashed him with its hammer was standing right there.

It was night, but the last train had not yet passed, and there were still a fair number of people coming and going from Ikebukuro Station.

People glanced suspiciously at the Dark Owl, but they figured the attacker wouldn't simply stand around in front of the station and treated it like some kind of tasteless attempt at an *OPD* promotional stunt.

There was one other reason that the people thought it was just a prank or a promotion.

"Th-th-th-th-there you are! H-hey, you guys, protect me!" Horada ordered. The fact that he said "protect me" instead of "attack" was an effective demonstration of his weakened state of mind.

"B-but, Mr. Horada, look... There!" said another one of his followers, pointing.

"H-huh?!"

There was another Dark Owl.

"A-and over there, too!"

There was another.

"L-look!"

And another.

Just in the vicinity of the station exit, there were at least five Dark Owls present.

Wh...wh-wh-what's going on?!

Horada was in a total panic. A follower said, "Th-there really are a bunch of them... I'm sorry, sir! I'm sorry for doubting you, Mr. Horada!"

"Huh? Oh yeah. Good. As long as you get it, that's all that matters."

There was a saying in Japan about lies that turn into truth. This was one truth he really didn't need. Horada began to wonder if he'd gotten himself into a situation that was truly dangerous.

"Wh-what should we do, Mr. Horada?!"

"Wh-what the hell *can* we do...?" he replied.

A few heartbeats later, after a quick scan of the entrance area, he spotted several more Dark Owls and turned on his heel with alacrity.

"Run for it!"

"Hey! W-wait up, Mr. Horada!"

Horada fled right back into the station, but because he was injured and could barely walk, his friends overtook him in moments.

"H-hey! No, hang on... Don't leave me behind, dammit!"

♂♀

Himeka's room

"What is this...?"

After preparing her stuff for school the next morning, Himeka spent some time looking on the Internet for more information on the street attacks. On a social media app called Twittia, she spotted some very odd information being traded.

At the moment, Ikebukuro was apparently overflowing with Dark Owls.

In fact, there were smartphone pics here and there, which suggested that there were quite a number of people dressed up as the Dark Owl, strolling about the area.

They didn't seem to be *doing* anything, least of all getting violent, but the reaction online suggested that people found it to be a very nasty prank.

"..."

Himeka got her cell phone so that she could call Yahiro about it. She scrolled through her call history until she found Yahiro's number, then pressed the call button.

"The number you have called is not currently available. Please try again later..."

"..."

Himeka had a bad feeling about this. She looked out the window.

In the distance, she could see the light from the Sunshine building. She balled her hands into fists with concern for her friend.

"I hope nothing's happened to Yahiro..."

♂♀

Kami-Ikebukuro—on the street

At that very moment, Yahiro's phone was not in any state to take a call—not after it had suffered a violent blow. It was no longer working.

It was a smartphone and not a kind that was especially resistant to impact, so he didn't know if it would ever work again. But he'd gotten a lesson from Kuon and taken out a cloud storage backup, so if he could get it repaired, he would probably be able to recover all his data.

The repairs would be costly, but at the moment, Yahiro wasn't worried about that.

He was too busy focusing on the threat of the *second* street attacker in front of them.

But the price of Yahiro's smartphone paid for Yumasaki's chance to dodge the attacker in the eleventh hour.

A few seconds earlier, a hammer was going to swing down upon his head—but Yahiro's phone hurtled at incredible speed and struck the weapon.

Knowing that he couldn't get there in time, Yahiro used the one thing on hand he could throw: his expensive phone.

It was a flat, rectangular device, not a conveniently shaped ball. Whether his successful strike was out of innate skill or just plain good luck, the phone hit its target square enough and hard enough that the hammer bounced back upward out of the way.

"..."

The second attacker looked toward Yahiro in apparent surprise— then craned their neck with suspicion.

Yumasaki, who'd slipped away from the attackers and brandished his fire extinguisher again, glanced at Yahiro and exclaimed with great surprise.

"...Did you *transform*?!"

As his words suggested, Yahiro was Yahiro, but he was not Yahiro.

He didn't want the attacker to see his face. Or if necessary, he did not want anyone else to see him committing great violence against the attacker.

This cowardly idea came from his conversation with Libei, when the other man suggested that a mysterious figure defeating the street attacker would remove all suspicion of gang warfare. So as he rushed over here, he'd taken out something he always kept in his bag.

It was a mysterious black fabric that had almost no weight at all.

The fabric formed a black mask and overcoat, a present from Celty Sturluson. In combination with his black pants, it meant Yahiro was almost entirely covered in black.

So if anything, he looked like a shadow man right now.

Writhing, flickering shadow that moved like dry ice wreathed Yahiro's body, as though it were competing with the Headless Rider's suit of darkness.

This figure looked far more alien than the attacker.

The latest urban legend of Ikebukuro, Snake Hands, was not just a formless legend. It was here on the street, taking actual form—to face off against the street attackers.

The irony was that he wore the mask of shadow as a result of his own cowardice, but it only gave the residential area a more distinct and memorable visual.

Two Dark Owls.

Snake Hands, the phantom.

And a civilian with a flame-throwing fire extinguisher.

Kadota showed up a few moments later, took in the scene around him, and uttered the only thing anyone could say about it.

"…What the fuck?"

♂♀

But while the situation might have appeared absurd, Yahiro's body was blaring with warning signals on the inside.

Is it possible I've been mistaken about this?

The concern shot through his body in the span of an instant.

This wasn't just some incident of a person attacking others on the street.

At first, he thought that the worst possible answer would be that it was part of a turf war between punks.

But what if the truth made that look like child's play?

What if these street attacks were something that had been intentionally orchestrated?

What if the person he was looking at wasn't even a real street attacker but something *else*?

Various possibilities crossed his mind, and a chill similar to pain shot through all of Yahiro's cells.

The reason was simple.

It was not because of the eeriness of seeing two attackers at once.

This was something that went beyond just the street attacks.

The problem was the second Dark Owl.

Something about the way it stood there and acted set Yahiro's entire being on edge.

"Ahyeeaaaahh!" The original attacker who had gone after Yumasaki let out a screech and jumped into motion.

"Oh! Hang on!" Yumasaki blurted out, trying to stop them—until the other attacker blocked his path. "Damn! Using clone techniques is no fair! I gotta sterilize you, impostor!"

He pulled the lever of his tool without a second thought.

If he'd used full pressure, the extinguisher was designed to spit fire between five and ten yards, but even Yumasaki had enough sense not to start a huge fire in this residential area.

Of course, it was tempting to say that he didn't have much sense for bringing a flame-throwing extinguisher into that residential area originally—or for creating a flame-throwing extinguisher in the first place. But that was one of the ways in which Yumasaki was missing a screw from the very beginning.

The moderated flame shot toward the second attacker, but they ducked down and actually slipped forward into the range of the flame.

"?!"

To Yumasaki's shock, the Dark Owl *slipped past* the flame. With inhuman speed and reflexes, they nimbly avoided the waves of fire and snuck right within reach of Yumasaki.

From his perspective, it was like the figure simply teleported toward him.

Could this be…?

He was inclined to compare it to some technique from anime or manga, but the attacker didn't give him enough time to think, attacking Yumasaki from below.

It was a rising uppercut.

An attack sure to knock him unconscious if it connected...

But just before the blow struck home, Yahiro kicked the arm out of the way from the side.

The kick threw off the path of the swing, causing the uppercut punch to only graze Yumasaki's cheek and slip past him.

...! I knew it!

That was all the confirmation he needed.

The Dark Owl he was now facing was an enemy on an *impossible level*.

Yahiro's kick was intended to bowl over his enemy sideways. But all it succeeded at doing was slightly budging the path of the punch.

This fighter had incredible core balance and powerful limbs. When he lived in Akita, Yahiro had to deal with people who had martial arts training—this opponent felt reminiscent of those sorts of opponents. However, while their general style might be similar, the difficulty couldn't be more different.

The self-styled martial artists back home broke down very easily, but the Dark Owl here didn't seem likely to back off from any number of kicks.

The alarms that had been sounding in Yahiro's mind were very similar to what he heard when facing off against Shizuo.

I'm scared.

I'm scared. I'm scared. I'm scared I'm scared I'm scared scared scared scared scaredscaredscaredscaredscared sc a r ed scared.

It's the same.

The same as with Shizuo.

He's strong. Strong strong strong.

This person might be able to kill *me.*

That moment of recognition caused fear to overtake his body.

For the first time in ages, a single sensation rose from his gut, overwhelming and undeniable: *I have to finish him off before he kills me.*

When he fought Shizuo, he didn't feel the same level of deadly malice. There was rage within the young man, that much was certain, and it was earned, but there was nothing like that from this figure.

It was as terrifying as a naked blade jutting out of the ground. One wrong step and everything would be over.

The identity of this Dark Owl didn't matter anymore.

"...Step back please," he said to Yumasaki, then produced his next attack.

It was a fierce chop toward the vicinity of the Dark Owl's throat.

But the Dark Owl did a huge backflip to avoid it, putting itself several yards away all at once.

It looked like the figure's upper half was bent backward at an angle over ninety degrees in the act of dodging the chop. The flexibility and control to take that into a backflip rather than straightening up was remarkable.

Ugh, I want to run away. I want to run away, Yahiro thought.

If he ran away and hid under his blanket and went to sleep, how reassured could he be about his safety?

They hadn't seen his face.

They didn't know his name.

That was the key to his security.

But if I run away now, he thought, gritting his teeth and stepping forward, *Yumasaki and Kadota are in big trouble. And even if we all escape...it just means someone else I care about might be next. And that's even more frightening than any of this.*

He drew that line in his mind and tightened the screws again.

Then he took a leap.

His feet launched him forward off the asphalt, attempting to catch his opponent off guard. Yahiro raced across the ground, feeling the fluid in his body collecting toward the back. He jumped at an angle.

His feet hit the side wall, as though he were running sideways, and he used that surface to leap to a height of ten feet. The idea was to zoom toward his target so he could kick that head like a soccer ball.

But the man ducked at the last second, avoiding the kick.

Yahiro's shoe grazed the top of the hood, sending a few fizzling and singed fibers flying into the air.

And without stopping, Yahiro deflected off the far wall, bouncing toward the Dark Owl with all his momentum.

It was a flurry of fists.

With all his blows, including elbows and kicks, Yahiro's opponent lost balance a number of times.

But in each case, they regained poise and flowed right into a smooth counterattack.

Yahiro's experience and instinct and reflexes helped him manage the counter, but it was enough to tell him that this fight was evenly matched.

If he lost his focus for even an instant, his foe would easily knock him unconscious. That was what had happened in the fight with Shizuo.

But this Dark Owl did not have Shizuo's strength, it seemed. Instead, whether natural or the product of fighting experience, Yahiro's opponent seemed to have an unerring sense of guesswork and deflection that made it impossible to land a good hit, and they could still fight back at times.

Think. Think, think, think.

He might not have Shizuo's strength, but he's got something *near its level!*

The fight felt life-threatening. And his foe still held a hammer; if that hammer hit him somewhere vital, it could be fatal.

I have to stop him from moving.

Despite the fever pitch of their combat, Yahiro was strangely calm.

Stop his legs.

Stop his arms.

Stop his thoughts.

Stop his senses.

Stop his breathing.

Stop his ___.

Time moved slowly.

Stop his ___.

It was a sensation he never felt when fighting the thugs in Akita.

Stop his ___.

Stop his heart.

As they traded blows, there was a brief moment when his hostility toward the opponent turned deadly.

Instantly, Yahiro's attacks got just a bit sharper, and he managed to land a punch to his enemy's face, which made the hood slip off a bit, revealing the lower half of the man's face. He appeared to be young, with a trail of blood flowing from his mouth. He was grinning.

Huh?

It made Yahiro wonder what his own face looked like right now.

I wonder why.

When it's so frightening... When I might die any moment now...

Conflicted and uncertain of how to feel, Yahiro was able to ascertain at least *one* thing: what kind of face he was making.

Am I...smiling?

♂♀

At that moment, Ikebukuro

"Y-yes! Got him!"

Ajimura stomped on the back of the fallen delinquent with triumph and yelled happily at the other Dark Owl.

"Ha! Ha-ha! Ha-haaa! Way to go, way to go!"

"..."

The other Dark Owl just stared at him in silence, but Ajimura chattered on without a care.

"Y-you're the one who helped me smash that Horada scumbag the other time! Weren't you? That was a big help! He actually had the gall to hit me! When *he's* the scumbag!"

"..."

The other one just stared, holding its hammer. For the first time, Ajimura felt a small amount of disquiet.

"H-hey, say something."

"..."

By way of an answer, the other one walked slowly toward him.

"...H-hey, is this a joke? You're not gonna get me next, are you? That's not funny!"

"..."

Still there was no answer.

Ajimura took his foot off the thug's back and inched away.

"H-hang on! Wait, please! Huh? Aren't you...on my side?"

"…"

"…! I am you! You are me! We're both the Dark Owl, aren't we?! *OPD* is the story of our lives, right! C'mon! We're both *OPD* fans; we should be getting along!"

"…"

The other Dark Owl did not react to his speech. They slowly, slowly closed the gap with Ajimura in silence.

Almost like the zombies that featured in *Owl of the Peeping Dead*.

"Aaah, aaaaah!"

When the Dark Owl's vibe matched with that of the zombies in his mind, Ajimura succumbed to the pressure and swung his hammer at the other one's head.

With an ugly crunch, it smashed in the hood covering the Dark Owl's skull.

"Eeep?!"

The hammer dented the other Owl's head much deeper than he expected, which filled Ajimura with sudden horror. He let go of the hammer and fell backward onto his butt. He looked upward, shivering, at the other Owl.

He'd certainly *felt* that head cave in.

It was a sensation he hadn't felt before. But with the hammer going that far in, the other person couldn't still be alive.

"Aaaaaah, it…it wasn't my fault. Y-you shouldn't have frightened me like that. You know? Da…za…zo…zwah…aaaaaaaaaaaah!!"

His stammered excuses switched into a scream of terror. The other Dark Owl, their head half crushed, began to move.

The second Owl took a smartphone from their pocket, typed a message into it, then showed Ajimura the screen.

"Sorry about that."

"…H-hwah?!"

"I don't really know that much about Owl of the Peeping Dead. *I was planning to see the movie, though,"* typed the other Dark Owl, despite their dented head. Ajimura could only open and close his mouth fruitlessly.

At that point, the other Dark Owl pulled back their hood, and Ajimura understood why the Dark Owl was able to move with their head crushed.

Because there was never any head there to begin with.

Shivering and rocking, Ajimura spoke the name of the creature aloud. "H...H-H-H...Headless...Rider!"

"This is for earlier," the Headless Rider typed, then transformed its hammer.

The bandages split and fell away, and the hammer underneath grew two sizes larger and transformed into a comically cartoonish bopping hammer, colored black.

She used the same hammer technique she'd tried out on her domestic partner, only ten times more powerful, slamming it into Ajimura's cheek—but as he fell unconscious, he had no clue of how she'd come to be there.

♂♀

Celty Sturluson was not human.

She was a type of fairy commonly known as a dullahan, found from Scotland to Ireland—a being that visits the homes of those close to death to inform them of their impending mortality.

The dullahan carried its own severed head under its arm, rode on a two-wheeled carriage called a Cóiste Bodhar pulled by a headless horse, and approached the homes of the soon to die.

Anyone foolish enough to open the door was drenched with a basin full of blood. Thus, the dullahan, like the banshee, made its name as a herald of ill fortune throughout European folklore.

Tonight, she wore a slightly different face.

She dressed herself in store-bought *kigurumi* pajamas, making herself look just like the Dark Owl street attacker.

♂♀

Several minutes later

"...I can't believe I got dragged into this farce."

She was in the corner of the park. Once she had confirmed there was no one else around, Celty checked up on the delinquent nearby—Kuon.

The unconscious street attacker was tied up with Celty's shadow, lying on the ground just as Kuon had been moments earlier.

In short, Kuon was a decoy.

He lured Ajimura, the street attacker, to a secluded place, where Celty, dressed as the street attacker, was supposed to get rid of him. The operation worked out just as planned.

Kuon "passed out," pretending to get hit by Celty, but now he was perfectly fine and cheery.

"Wow, that worked out perfectly. Thank you! Is him knowing you're the Headless Rider gonna be a problem?"

Kuon had called Celty up because he had an idea of who the culprit was. She showed up at the meeting spot, where he gave her a set of Dark Owl pajamas.

"See, if it gets out that the Headless Rider defeated the attacker, it means he's going to have a big grudge against you, won't he? Plus, if the Dark Owl captures the Dark Owl...it kind of repairs the Dark Owl's reputation, don't you think?" he told her.

She didn't think it would work out that cleanly, but he was the one who hired her, so she decided to go along with the plan as he hoped.

In any case, everything else was a trivial matter after stopping the attacker's reign of terror.

As a result, the street attacker himself found out she was the Headless Rider, but Celty didn't seem to be that bothered by it.

"It'll be fine. I'm used to being hated by weirdos like him."

"Hmm, okay. Sounds like a pain, though."

"But you're not disappointed by this?"

"Huh?" Kuon said, feigning ignorance.

"You put together the Dark Owl kigurumi for me," she pointed out. *"You were hoping to get some footage of the Dark Owl capturing the Dark Owl, weren't you?"*

"...Well, damn. Where do you think I'd be taping something like this...?"

"That pen in your chest pocket is a pen-sized digital video camera, isn't it? They sell them online now. I was really excited about my favorite old spy movies coming to life, so I bought a few, along with a glasses-frame camera."

Kuon considered joking about what use the Headless Rider would have for a glasses camera, but this probably wasn't the time.

Instead, he admitted, "Okay, fine, you got me. I had a number of cameras ready; plus, I hired some folks to keep anyone unrelated out of the area. I also had a cell phone camera recording from a distance."

"Don't act like you should be proud of it."

"...Are you angry?"

"I'm not angry. I'm just giving you a warning that this isn't very cool of you," Celty typed, then shrugged her shoulders to look like she was exhaling. *"You shouldn't underestimate other people. Anyone could predict you might try something like this. You're free to use me in your moneymaking schemes, but don't spread any videos that reveal my identity or cause people to mistakenly think I'm a kidnapper."*

"...In that case, I'll edit the part where your head gets smashed."

"I can't believe you still want to use that footage!"

"I'll make it up to you with extra pay. Please, just let me do this," Kuon insisted without a hint of shame. Celty felt like she was getting a better and better grasp of what kind of person he was.

"It's fine if you use other people. I happen to believe that people get by in life by using one another, but it goes both ways. I knew someone who tried to always be the manipulator, but only a special few can pull it off, and everyone hates them."

"...You mean Izaya Orihara?"

"You know him?" asked Celty, surprised.

Her reaction was not so much about Kuon knowing Izaya—but about the way that his smile vanished as soon as he spoke the name aloud and how his eyes brimmed with an endless chilly rage.

"We have a history..."

"Then you should get it, shouldn't you? He's not a person you want to emulate."

"He's a real son of a bitch and the one person I hate above all others," Kuon said, gritting his teeth. For some reason, he looked chagrined. "But even a guy like him can do good things for people... That's all."

The look on his face left Celty speechless for a bit. She ultimately decided to change the topic rather than pursue this one further.

"I see. Well, I won't ask more. I gave you my warning. But that wasn't my concern anyway."

"…Then what is?"

"How did you know he was the culprit?" she asked, her biggest question at the moment. How did Kuon know that this man was the one responsible? The decoy tactic wouldn't have worked at all if he didn't know this already.

"It wasn't me. It was my sister."

"What do you mean?"

Kuon looked a little guilty as he described his family's business. "Sis's message boards picked up this guy who was getting really worked up once the street attacks started happening. He was posting all the time, saying, 'The Dark Owl is a good guy; he's cleaning up all the scum in our city.' And he would make fake accounts that agreed with him and spam the same comments over and over. Of course, Sis could see he had the same IP address the whole time…"

"And that was Ajimura?"

"Yes. Out of all the sites my sister runs, one of them is an aggregate for *OPD* information, and the guy on there had the exact same address as the admin for this really infamous so-called fan site. We did some research, and after the incident with that Horada guy recently, he was out there stressing that Horada was a delinquent well before the cops even announced it was him."

"He seems like an idiot," Celty typed frankly.

Kuon smirked and nodded. "Well, when you get to know him, yeah. Maybe the fact that he's so stupid is how he got to attacking people on the street in the first place," he noted dryly.

"Is that all?" Celty asked.

"…About what?"

"If that's all there was to him, I feel like you would have let him continue or had someone like Yahiro handle it."

It was hard to tell because it was just writing, but Kuon sensed a dry sort of tone all the same.

"What are you trying to say, Celty?"

"I'm saying…something happened that either you or your sister didn't expect… Am I wrong?"

"Something unexpected...? It doesn't have to be unexpected for us to want to catch a violent criminal. Although I guess I admit it was a surprise to me that a guy who was being a pest on one of my sister's sites turned out to be the one responsible."

Kuon blithely chatted on, delivering scattered impressions of the case, but Celty put a pin in his reminiscence with a direct question.

"When I was dressed up as the Dark Owl, he said something like, 'You helped me earlier'... What did that mean?"

"Hey, I wish I knew. I suppose the rumors are true, and there are copycat attackers out there, too. Maybe he was one of them. In any case, he was still one of the attackers," Kuon stated, setting a foot on Ajimura's back. "If there's anything I can do, it's hand him over to Karisawa and her friends."

He chuckled, then took out his phone—and placed a call to Karisawa's number.

It seemed very much like he was trying to distract Celty from her line of questioning.

"...Ah, hello, is this Karisawa? Hi, it's Kuon Kotonami."

"Huh?! Kuocchi?! What's up? I thought you said you were busy today."

"Actually, it just wrapped up... Me and Celty caught the attacker."

"Huh?!"

"I'd like to hand him over to you, so I was hoping to ask for your buddy...uhhh...the driver of the van, if he could come and pick us up?"

"Um...well...that would be fine...but what's going on?"

"Wh...what do you mean?"

"I mean, I'm with Togucchi right now, see..."

She was apparently talking on the phone while running, because there were footsteps and heavy panting as she spoke.

"Togucchi just called Dotachin...and he said Yappy...I mean, Mizuchi? He's fighting with the street attacker now..."

"...Huh?"

A few seconds after hanging up, still entirely baffled, Kuon got a call from a different number.

"...Tatsugami?"

Once again, he was confused, by the timing in this case, but he answered the call anyway.

"...Hello?"

"Ah, Kotonami? Have you seen what's going on online?"

"Online? No."

"They say there are Dark Owls all over the city..."

"...Huuuh?!"

A few minutes later, Kuon had scrolled through his timeline enough to be reeling with the news.

Celty stuck out her smartphone to show him a question. *"What's up? Something else 'unexpected' happen?"*

"...No. It's nothing." He smiled, pretending.

"It's harder than you think to get people to act how you want," she typed. *"Izaya didn't actually control anyone. He loved and accepted the results, no matter what they were, and that just made it look like he wanted it to turn out that way... In any case, the results were always a pain in the ass."*

Oddly enough, despite claiming it was a "pain in the ass," Celty did not seem to be all that upset. Kuon gave her a piercing glare, then opened his mouth.

"Don't act like you know what..."

Then he paused, stopped himself, and looked away uncomfortably.

"No...maybe you're right..."

He fell silent and resumed looking at his online feeds.

Celty did not criticize or comfort him any further. She knew that saying anything more would indeed be acting like she knew what she was talking about.

And what she knew about was Izaya Orihara's past, not whatever was happening in the present.

♂♀

On the street, Kami-Ikebukuro

"..."

By the time Karisawa and Saburo reached the scene, the fight had entered a kind of stalemate.

Both sides had launched into a series of attacks, neither one finding a proper finisher. At the moment, they'd taken up some distance and were watching and waiting out the other side.

Yumasaki pointed his nozzle at the attacker, thinking this might be his big chance, but Kadota held out a hand to stop him.

"Don't be an idiot. He'll just dodge it and take advantage of Yahiro instead," he muttered. Yumasaki saw the sense in that and lowered the extinguisher.

Saburo came up behind them and saw a silhouette that resembled Yahiro.

"H-hey, what's going on here?" he exclaimed. "Huh...? What is that? Why's he wearing that dark mask... Hang on... Isn't that Celty's shadow...?"

"A transforming hero?! Incredible! If this were a *tokusatsu* show, that'd be some really high-end production! Just look at the way the shadow moves!"

"Uh, hang on, Karisawa. I need a second. I'm having trouble processing it...," said Saburo, getting confused by the way she was describing the scene.

Then he heard the familiar sound of a siren.

"Oh, it's the cops."

Someone in the neighborhood must have noticed the commotion from their window and called it in. At any rate, there were police sirens coming this way—that much was clear.

In reaction, the Dark Owl looked at Yahiro with disappointed longing—then grinned through the gap in the ripped hood and withdrew from the scene.

"Huh?! He ran away!" blurted out Yumasaki, fumbling with his fire extinguisher. He did not get the chance to blow fire at the man, though.

To his shock, the Dark Owl raced directly up the wall bordering a private home, then jumped to the first-floor roof, then the second, like some kind of wild animal. Within a few moments, he was on the other side of the roof and gone.

"Wh-what is that guy, a wildcat?!" exclaimed Saburo.

"Maybe...the real Dark Owl came to life out of the movie...," Yumasaki murmured absentmindedly.

Then Saburo noticed the fire extinguisher in his hands and yelped, "Hey, Yumasaki! Put that thing away! We gotta go!"

"What?! But the attacker—!! Th-there's another one! They ran off!"

"That comes later! None of this matters if we get arrested first!"

While the others bickered and shouted, Yahiro continued to stare at the roof where the Dark Owl disappeared.

"He...ran...away...?"

When that realization hit him, Yahiro felt a fresh wave of sweat seep from his skin.

He couldn't tell whether it was a cold sweat of fear or simply the heat from fierce exertion. He was still in a state of bewilderment, unable to process what he'd just experienced. Then a familiar voice said, "Hey, Yahiro! What are you doing? You gotta move, too!"

"Oh...right!"

He saw the flashing red lights of the police cars in the distance and turned on his heel and ran.

As he rushed down the street, he removed the mask and suit of shadow, folding them up into a ball he tucked under his arm. In his heart, he felt a tiny bit of relief.

The threat was gone.

But the fear was not. It hadn't completely vanished.

Perhaps the attacker just pretended to run away and was setting up an ambush elsewhere.

Perhaps the police had actually spotted Yahiro and set up a trap.

Perhaps he'd get scolded by Saburo and kicked out of the apartment.

Among those typical fears, there was a new one, something freshly sprung from the soil of his psyche.

He was afraid of himself for feeling an elation during his battle that was even greater than during his fight against Shizuo Heiwajima.

Despite being in the midst of combat, he was aware enough to reflect on himself and feel uneasy.

So Yahiro fled toward the main street in a mild panic.

And that was when he heard a voice behind him say, "Yahiro."

Spinning around defensively, prepared for anything, he saw something hurtling toward him.

A knife?! Acid?! A bomb?!

Many possibilities passed through his mind, but his visual cortex identified the object right as his reflexes kicked in and caught the smartphone.

"You forgot that on the ground back there. It seems broken. Is that gonna be a problem right now?" Yahiro looked at the other person, who was shrugging, with confusion.

"Kuronuma…? What are you doing here?"

♂♀

Ikebukuro—on the street

"Wh-what should we do, Mr. Horada?!"

"Look, just get us away from the station! It's one o' those, uh…strategic retreats! Yeah! Then we just gotta figure out somethin' else!" Horada shouted, sitting in the passenger seat of his follower's car and trembling with the pain.

He'd managed to get through the station to the parking lot. Now they were driving away, trying to put distance between them and the building. They were taking smaller side routes to avoid the traffic on the main streets.

"Dammit… What the hell was up with them?! These guys are worse than gangbangers!" Horada exclaimed. Then his phone went off. "What?! Who the hell is calling me…now…?"

He trailed off and went pale when he saw the name Izumii on the screen. He answered the call.

"H-hello, Izumii! It's Horada!"

"So here's the question."

"Y-yes, sir?"

"Why would young Horada, who needed a full week in the hospital to recover, already be out of said hospital?"

Izumii's quiz set Horada's teeth rattling. Whenever Izumii started doing his quiz routine, it tended to be when he had more screws loose than usual.

If he played it poorly, he might end up worse than hospitalized. But Horada couldn't come up with a clever answer to the question.

"Well? What's up with the attacker?"

"W-well…"

♂♀

Youko Shirobishi ran and ran.

Oh, dammit. It's all over. All over. Shit! Shit, shit, shit, shit, shit.

She was in utter despair—but not because her voice had been overheard and maybe the police could find her from that.

It was because of the dark shadow that appeared just before she took off.

It wasn't at all like the black costumes—more like shadow itself that turned into fabric and writhed on its own. First, it was the Headless Rider, then that bizarre other person, showing up to interfere with her mission.

Oh, it's all over. Ikebukuro is done for. The gates to hell have been opened. And now the devils are here! It wasn't me. It wasn't my fault. It was those scumbags. Those scum-sucking, evil bastards, lower than maggots, impure cretins who exude filth worse than the refuse of *%&^, have accepted evil into their hearts and opened the gates to hell!

This city is finished. It must be finished—by my hand.

Nooo, there's still time. I must save them by my hand. Burn them all. Burn all the heretical books. I'll buy a lighter at the store and burn all of Ikebukuro. Burn, baby, burn, baby. Burn, burn, burn.

All by my hand, my hand, me, me, me, me, memememememememememememememe…

She ran on in a demented charge, saliva dripping from the corner of her mouth.

There was clearly something wrong with her. Maybe it was fear, or a new mission she'd found for herself, or perhaps some other reason.

The chaos paradoxically filled her with joy, and she felt no fatigue anymore. She was running for the sake of Ikebukuro.

The woman was running, running straight toward her shining future…

…into the path of a car that struck her from the side.

♂♀

"What's wrong? That sounded pretty loud," Izumii said through the phone.

Horada was silent with agony, waves of pain surging through his entire body, thanks to the impact from the car hitting something.

"It was…just the car…"

"Uh, Mr. Horada? L-look at that…," said the driver, who stopped the car in the street. There was a person crumpled on the ground nearby.

Are you fucking kidding me?! I don't need any more cops in my life! I didn't do this one! I didn't do it!

He scrambled out of the car as hastily as he could, clutching his cell phone. At the very least, he wanted to see if the person was dead or alive.

"…Burn it…burn them. Kill the scum, the scum, the scum," the Dark Owl muttered, twitching with a bandaged hammer in their hands. Horada's eyes bulged.

"Hey, Horada. What's going on? Talk to me," said the voice on the phone, bringing him back to his senses. Horada quickly lifted it to his ear.

"S-sorry about that! We got a situation here!"

"Just answer the question. You dealt with your attacker, right? Huh?"

"Y-yes!"

"…What?"

"Of course we did, Mr. Izumii! We found the street attacker, and we made quick work of 'em! We'll take 'em to you right now. Hope you're ready, sir!"

♂♀

"Nn…huh?"

When Ajimura opened his eyes next, he was inside someone else's van.

"Ah. Rise and shine. Or in Dark Owl fashion, should I say, 'Welcome back to the land of the living'?"

"Not that you'll be seeing anything but a prison cell for a long time."

He was greeted by a man with narrow eyes holding a bucket and a woman dressed in black with a battery-powered soldering iron.

"Wh…what…? Who are you people?!" He realized his hands were bound. He writhed and rocked around.

"Whoa, don't struggle so much. The Dark Owl is supposed to be cool and collected," the young woman said.

"You've got to keep your body temperature down, like the real thing." A moment later, the narrow-eyed man shoveled some dry ice from his bucket down into Ajimura's clothes.

"Aaaaaaah?! Ah…aaaah!" he screamed.

"I'll admit, I'm shocked you were attacking people on the street while carrying your ID around, but seeing your name was an even bigger shock. The admin of that infamous *OPD* site turned out to be the actual culprit?"

"But considering how terrible that site's reputation is, it's not *that* surprising. Though I wouldn't have expected you were using your actual name to run it."

"Wha…? Terrible reputation?!" Ajimura shrieked. "Screw you! I did this…to protect *OPD*! I was cleaning up the scum of this city like Horada and Shizuo Heiwajima! I was protecting the Dark Owl's reputation!"

The man and woman looked at each other—then sighed with matching expressions of utter exhaustion.

"Cleaning up the scum to prove that you're good? Don't you realize that this completely contradicts the whole theme of *OPD*? He agonizes over killing zombies and refuses to consider himself the good guy when he defeats the bad guys!"

"I mean, even the Dark Owl, the villain of the show, talks about how evil he is before he does evil deeds. What show have you been watching? You're even dumber than the dumbest fans."

"Shut up! That's all just surface-level stuff they crammed in there! WWW only wrote it that way to suck up to the commercial industry and get their series made! You'd have to be a total amateur to miss the *secret, real themes* that exist behind all of that!" Ajimura shouted, counter to all logic.

The narrow-eyed man held him down.

"Gaaah… What are you…? Aaaaaaah!"

By being pressed against the ground, the dry ice inside of his suit burned his skin. He screamed and screamed, but the man and woman weren't done with him.

"Well, we aren't actually fans. See, a real fan wouldn't try to solve their favorite series' problems using violence. But we will," the man said.

"That's right. You know, at first I thought you couldn't really see the true story...but then again, maybe you knew that the Dark Owl was originally designed to be blind?" The woman reached closer to his eye with the soldering iron.

"N-no, stop... Stop, stop, stop—aaaaaaaaaaaaaahhhh!"

The rear door of the van opened just before the tip of the iron touched his eyeball. For a moment, Ajimura thought that help had come for him—but when he saw the cold look in the eyes that met his own, that futile hope was crushed.

The man who had opened the door wore a bandanna around his head. He sighed and spoke to the man and woman.

"Hey...don't get our goals here mixed up," said Kadota through the back door. Yumasaki and Karisawa hastened to explain.

"It's fine, it's fine. We just want to find out how many others there are with him."

"Come on—you could stand to trust us a little bit!"

"...Well, if you say so. But as soon as you get the information you want, we're handing him to the cops. Don't forget that," Kadota warned before turning to Saburo outside. "What's up with Yahiro?"

"I sent him back home before we picked up the attacker. Didn't want him to see *this*."

"I can't believe he turned out to be this Snake Hands people are talking about."

"...Man, I don't even know what's going on anymore," Saburo grumbled, exhausted.

"You gonna give him a lecture tomorrow?" Kadota asked.

"No? Maybe my family will, but when it comes to fighting, I don't have the right to scold anyone else." Saburo shrugged. Yahiro's face appeared in his mind, and he looked up at the sky, grimacing.

*   *   *

"There's just one thought on my mind: It's a violent world out there. The only thing I care about is that he goes right back to our apartment without any detours, safe and sound."

♂♀

Rooftop of Kuon's apartment—night

"Shit…the plan's a bust. Everything failed…" Kuon leaned on the railing around the rooftop, muttering angrily. "What the hell…? What was with all those Dark Owls showing up around the station…? That wasn't a part of the plan. Who the hell were they…?"

Whose work was that?

The only thing he could think of was maybe that growing online group, the Underars, or some other group of pranksters doing a bit of a public art performance.

In any case, this had totally changed Ikebukuro's impression of the Dark Owl. If that lessened the impact of the video of the street attacker and Headless Rider, then that was that. But it was something Kuon couldn't accept.

My plans are all shot. I should have had an easier time using the attacker to my own ends…

He clicked his tongue and sighed. Amid the blended sound of his breath and the wind blowing between the buildings, he heard the door opening behind him.

"…Sis?"

She was the only one who knew he was up here. But it wasn't Nozomi.

"Yahiro…?"

It was Yahiro Mizuchi, dressed in his plain clothes, looking the way he always did.

"What are you doing here?"

"I came to visit, and Nozomi said you were up here."

"Look, if you want to talk, you could just call."

"Sorry. My phone is busted," Yahiro explained simply.

Kuon chuckled. "What do you mean…? I guess you fought the attacker?"

"Well, I was fighting against the Dark Owl, and he was tough. I couldn't tell who it was on the inside, but it seemed like Kuronuma knew."

"…Hang on—why are you mentioning Aoba?" Kuon asked, confused but still smiling.

"He said that out of all those Dark Owls who showed up in Ikebukuro today…almost all of them were *really* Blue Squares."

"…Huh?! What the hell does that mean?! Why would he…?"

"He said he wanted to mess with you."

"?!" Kuon was stunned, baffled.

"Hey, Kuon…"

Yahiro asked the question on his mind the same way he would say any other thing.

"Did you *always* know that this Ajimura guy was the attacker?"

♂♀

"I've got the attacker, like we discussed. So I handed them over to Kuon Kotonami, a member of the Blue Squares. Whatever happens next isn't my problem. I've paid you back for one favor," read Celty's message.

Aoba smirked. "So that's your angle."

She did, in fact, fulfill his request. She'd probably done it this way because she detected the uncomfortable relationship between Kuon and the Blue Squares.

"So Celty knew that Kuon was one of us…? She's oddly perceptive about subtle things like that."

"What are we gonna do about Kuon, man?" asked one of his friends. "He went too far this time, didn't he?"

"He could've destroyed the Blue Squares' reputation with this stunt," said another.

But Aoba cheerfully replied, "It's cool. We took a worse hit to our reputation by choice today, didn't we?"

"Oh yeah, I saw it made the news… I wonder how much Kuon's sister will pay for the exclusive scoop from us?"

"Yoshikiri did a good job on this one. Gotta send him a call of gratitude later." Aoba cackled. The group continued to discuss the job they performed.

"I wish I could see the look on Kuon's face right now."

"He probably thinks it was the Underars's work, not us. I bet he never considered the possibility that we'd gone over his head and set up the whole fake with Nozomi herself."

Aoba envisioned the look of gnashed teeth and frustration on his younger acquaintance's face and sipped his beverage.

"But as for what happens to him…I guess it depends on his friend."

"I *did* tell the kid everything Kuon got up to."

♂♀

"So Aoba…realized everything I was doing while it was happening?"

"Apparently, he's been monitoring you ever since the faked kidnapping last month or so. In secret. He watches a lot of stuff online, I guess."

"Whoa, that's freaky. What is he, a stalker?" Kuon said, trying to pass it off as a joke, but with as stone-faced as Yahiro was, his smile quickly faded away.

"…So what did he say about me?"

"Hmm…I don't know the full details, but he said everything fell into place in the last few days. Most likely, the attacker you knew about was this Ajimura person. And he thought that once you knew about *him*, you were working to blow it up into something bigger after that."

"…"

"He said that on Ajimura's site, there was someone pretending to be in with the group, handing out all kinds of details on delinquents and thugs. They were getting the folks riled up about Horada and some other rough types. Aoba said that was probably you."

He was right.

Kuon learned about Ajimura in the way that he'd told Celty he did. However, the timing was off. His sister had told him that Ajimura was fishy before he'd made the contract with Yumasaki and Karisawa.

He'd known who was responsible for the attacks. At the time, he asked himself, *Can I use that to my advantage to gain something? Or can I somehow manipulate the attacker's actions to make him attack specific people?*

Kuon had never had *a goal* in mind.

If anything, he wanted to try accurately controlling the street attacker's patterns.

That had been Kuon's biggest objective: to see whether he was capable of wielding that power or not.

He'd considered it a good test case.

He'd wanted to see if he had what it took to *be Izaya Orihara.*

With that thought in his mind once again, Kuon stopped smiling and glared at Yahiro. "Yeah, that's right."

"..."

"I knew long before Golden Week. What's more, I'm the one who egged that guy on to get him to attack Horada."

Up to that point, it had gone entertainingly to plan.

Kuon accepted the offer from Yumasaki and Karisawa, playing ignorant despite knowing who was responsible, and then he offered the job to Yahiro.

He also succeeded at sending the attacker after Horada, who seemed the most likely to interfere with the Blue Squares and Yahiro doing their job. It was almost like rigging a match; if Yahiro captured the attacker while acting as Snake Hands, it would help sell the name, and he'd be able to play that so Horada owed him a favor.

And that was when things went off the rails; a third party had interfered.

Another attacker appeared and helped beat Horada. The identity of this person didn't matter. The problem was that someone outside of his control inflicted their influence upon Ajimura.

Sensing danger, Kuon decided to withdraw his influence and observe for a bit.

Next, Ajimura sought out Shizuo Heiwajima. Kuon waited, not interfering, for Ajimura to attack Shizuo.

Of course, Ajimura would fail to do anything to him. And if he got smashed instead, Kuon could just hand him over to Yumasaki and Karisawa and complete the contract.

But Ajimura did not attack Shizuo. He attacked his superior at work, Tom Tanaka.

Kuon was there observing at the time, and that was when he determined that Ajimura could not be controlled anymore.

And that was why he used Celty to eliminate Ajimura at the soonest opportunity.

"Well? If this is all true, what do you think?" Kuon asked, challenging Yahiro.

He probably could have lied and talked his way out of the situation, but he didn't know how much evidence Aoba Kuronuma might have of what he was doing, so it would probably be wasted effort.

"If, as you claim, I knew who the attacker was and stood back in silence while he went after Horada and Shizuo Heiwajima's friend, what are you going to do about it?"

That's right.

I decided I wanted to be like Izaya Orihara. Why do I have to care about how Yahiro sees me?

Shouldn't I expect to be loathed, despised, disdained? In fact—yeah. If I'm Izaya, then he must be my Shizuo Heiwajima.

That works. That's not bad.

If the two of them ended up locked in a battle to the death right now, Kuon wouldn't care. Or at least, that was what he told himself as he awaited his answer.

However...

"What a relief."

"...Huh?"

"I just wanted to confirm things—that's all. If it's true, that's cool. Thanks," Yahiro said, reassured.

Kuon's mouth dropped. Then he gnashed his teeth with irritation and snapped, "How is that cool? What did you even come all this way for?"

Yahiro's tone of voice was the same as if they were discussing some mundane daily topic. "I was thinking, if it wasn't true, I'd have to go right back to Kuronuma and tell him it wasn't true."

"...Huh?"

It was an answer so far out of the expected that Kuon couldn't even be annoyed anymore. But he understood once Yahiro continued.

"It hurts to have mistakes spread like that. But if it's true, that's cool.

If it's something you wanted to have happen, I'm not going to poke my nose in your business."

Yahiro led a solitary childhood, all because of the stories that spread about his "monstrous" nature, something he never wanted for himself. That's where he was coming from.

Did he...really come here...just for that?

"Is that all you wanted, man?"

"About what?"

"You've got a sick bastard like me right in front of you, and you have the power to do something about it, and you're just going to let it all slide?! Like it's nothing?!"

"..."

"Or..."

Kuon came to a stop and clamped his mouth shut.

What...was I just about to say? "Or...do you not care about me at all?"

When he realized how close he'd been to saying those words, Kuon truly paled.

In the silence that followed, Yahiro considered the words that *did* get said—and put into words the thoughts he could consolidate.

"Uh...Kuon, you're trying to be like this Izaya Orihara guy, right?"

"Sis just had to go and tell you... What about it?"

"Isn't that kind of a waste?"

"...Huh? What does that mean?" Kuon snapped, his brow creased. He stepped closer to Yahiro. He knew that he didn't stand a chance in a fight, but this was a line that had been crossed for him. "You think I'm *wrong* to do it? You think I'm wrong for wanting to save my sister?"

"I don't think that's wrong. But I think you're doing it the wrong way."

"..." Yahiro's bluntness rendered Kuon speechless.

"I can't explain it very well...but it's something I've been thinking about... You said she's been through some tough times since Izaya Orihara vanished, right? So you want to be Izaya Orihara to help get her back to the way she used to be...right?"

"...Right."

"But what will that do if you end up dying?"

"...Huh?"

The question caught Kuon like a sucker punch, like he lost the air in his lungs for a moment.

Yahiro thought hard, choosing his words very carefully. "If you're gone, then won't the same thing happen to your sister as when Izaya Orihara was gone? How is she supposed to be happy without you around...?"

"..."

"So if you want her to be able to survive on her own after you're gone...then I don't think you should try to be like this Izaya Orihara guy."

It didn't seem like Yahiro was sure of what he was saying; he sounded so hesitant, as if he was afraid he might be incorrect. But even still, Yahiro was being honest about how he felt.

"I don't think I'm explaining it very well...but I think you'll have to be someone *even more amazing* than Izaya Orihara. You'll have to be someone who can make your sister happy in the truest sense."

After he finished, he tilted his head to the side, as if asking himself, *Is that really right?* Maybe there was a better answer.

Kuon watched him soundlessly. Eventually, the irritation faded from his features, and a little smile appeared in its place.

"...Enough. Go home."

"Oh, sorry. I guess I'm being weird, huh?"

"Yeah. So leave. I told you, I hate that goody-two-shoes side of you."

"...Okay. Sorry."

Yahiro was as expressionless as usual, but there *was* a subtle note of regret there. He turned his back on Kuon.

"Ah..."

Kuon was going to say something to him, but he couldn't find the words. Once he could tell that Yahiro wasn't going to slow down or stop, the fake smile vanished from Kuon's face, and his eyes turned mournful.

"...Wait," he said.

"What?"

When Yahiro turned around, Kuon was back to his usual smirking self. And in his casual way, he said, "What did you say the other time? You're always ready to hit me if you need to?"

"Yeah."

In his usual way, Kuon gave him the go-ahead.

"Now's the time. You gotta hit me to stop me."

"Got it."

In the next moment, Yahiro's fierce punch, as practiced as a pro boxer's, smashed into Kuon's right cheek, which was pointed just a little bit off center.

He hurtled backward spectacularly, smashing back first into the fence around the roof.

His conscious mind sank into darkness before it could register any pain.

♂♀

Twenty minutes later

When Kuon awoke, the first thing he noticed was the dull but fierce pain that enveloped his face.

The stars were out in the sky above, but the neon lights of the city blocked them, so it wasn't exactly a curtain of starlight overhead. He looked to the side, where sitting next to him was Yahiro, his back against the fence.

"You okay?"

"Ow, damn…"

Kuon tried to move, but it sent pain through his face. The sour, rusty taste of blood was in his mouth.

"You don't know…how to…go easy?"

"Nope. You were smiling, but your eyes said you were serious. So I thought, I need to take it seriously, too," Yahiro admitted.

Kuon put up with the pain in order to smile. "If your aim was just a little worse, I could've been dead…"

He spat something out into his hand. Along with a lot of blood, there were two pieces of teeth.

"They're broken."

"Yeah, you should go see a dentist," Yahiro said, rubbing the back of his hand. He had plenty of scars there.

Whether or not Kuon realized they were the marks from the broken teeth of people Yahiro punched, he grunted and complained, "Ugh... gah... Damn, man... You're really clumsy, you know that?"

Yahiro tilted his head and replied, "So are you, Kotonami."

"...Listen, man... After you've just beat the crap out of a guy to prove your friendship, it's kinda weird to call me by my last name. Don't sound so stiff."

"Is that how it works?"

"That's exactly how it works." Kuon grimaced through the pain but smiled at Yahiro anyway.

Yahiro considered this seriously. "All right. Then I'll just call you Kuon." With the same level of gravity, he continued, "I wonder if my friendship with Himeka will get closer someday."

"Uh...I dunno... Don't get *too* close."

"Oh...sorry. I don't know why you would be angry about it, though," Yahiro said, deflated.

Despite the pain, Kuon could only smile. He felt that if he let the smile leave his face, he would start crying.

The awkward boy just stared up at the faded, murky stars and smiled for all he was worth.

EPILOGUE

EPILOGUE

The next day—Shinra's apartment

It was midday after the weeklong holiday.

The afternoon variety shows announced that *three* street attackers had been arrested.

Two of them were copycats. One was a self-styled *OPD* fan who was hated by most other fans because of his extremist nature. The other was a woman who attacked *OPD* online and delivered various statements about the harm it posed to media companies for dissemination. The police were continuing their investigation into the woman, whom they believed might have coconspirators among her organization.

They were both injured and terrified and making bizarre statements like, "The Headless Rider is a street attacker" and "The devil showed up," so the investigation was taking into account the possibility that they were under the influence of illicit drugs of some kind.

But what really shocked the audience was the fact that the police investigation turned up the "original" attacker, as well.

The culprit was a new hostess at a club, who learned that the man who'd given her the most humiliating rejection of her life was romantically involved with another hostess there. So she grabbed some clothes at home that would hide her face and attacked the two of them.

"And once the true culprit is found, it turns out to be something

frivolous like this," typed Celty, dropping her shoulders like she was sighing.

"It wasn't the influence of manga or any nonsense like that. Just generic human jealousy. These things can be scary," Shinra said.

"But still, the woman was an OPD fan, right? Does that mean people will take it out on OPD after all?"

"I'm not sure. The two copycats both said they had the idea after seeing it reported on the media, so if the media tries to bash it too hard, that blame will come back around to them. I'm guessing it'll get swept under the rug. For one thing, the leader of the most extreme anti-*OPD* groups was one of the people doing the attacks."

"It's an ugly world out there. But I guess you're right. Just because the first person to start doing this was a hostess doesn't mean society's going to go on an anti-hostess screed," Celty typed, causing Shinra to laugh.

"Yeah, that's right. If they want a target to blame, it's human jealousy. It's the original human sin. Even I suffer from it."

"If I cheated on you, would you dress up in cosplay and beat people up?"

"I'd never do that. And I've calmed down a lot in the last few days," he reassured her. It was true that his manner was much gentler now.

"Then what would you do?" Celty asked.

"...I'd cry really hard. Just wail so loudly. There would be a fully grown man standing outside Ikebukuro Station in the middle of the day, bawling his eyes out and calling your name over and over."

"You're going to make everyone feel bad! Don't do that! Anyway...I get the sense we've had this conversation before...," Celty typed, but she felt relieved on the inside.

Things had been so chaotic since they came back from vacation. Maybe life was finally returning to normal for them.

On the TV, the news was talking about the arrest of the attackers, while online, people were going nuts over the group of Dark Owls that had showed up around Ikebukuro Station.

As she read an article about it, she asked Shinra, *"Who do you suppose did this? They didn't hurt anyone, and they ran off when the police showed up, so I guess it was just a prank."*

Shinra thought it over, scowled slightly, then guessed. "It was probably Aoba's group, right? From what you say, the Blue Squares are working with some online news portal to drum up fake stories. Wouldn't this count?"

Shinra's supposition was exactly correct, though neither of them had the evidence on hand to know it was true.

"Maybe it's some kind of public art project from the Underars."

"I suppose it's the work of Bannanjin, the demonic hammer..."

"Y-you don't think it's an alien conspiracy, do you?"

They traded different ideas, until the thought of Kuon drifted through Celty's mind.

He sure managed to screw everything up this time. I suppose he enjoys conspiracies, too. Between Izaya, Mikado, Aoba, and Kuon, what is it with Raira Academy and attracting guys who fancy themselves masterminds?

Anyway, Kuon is sweet and harmless compared to Izaya. After all, he and Shizuo wrecked up the town ever since their high school days...

At that thought, Celty's mind went blank.

"I forgot about Shizuo!"

"Huh?"

"I handed the attacker over to Karisawa and Yumasaki!"

The relaxed feeling she had just moments ago was totally gone, and Celty slumped onto the sofa.

"Oh, geez... How should I apologize to him...?"

♂♀

Raira Academy rooftop—after school

"You look sleepy, Yahiro."

"Do I?"

"You do," said Himeka, her face blank.

They were sitting near the edge of the roof, where Yahiro was explaining everything that happened. He didn't mention Kuon, but he described in full detail everything regarding the fight against the street attacker.

"Uh-huh...but how did you know that woman was the attacker?"

"Well, she was looking our way, and there was this, like, *hatred* in her manner…like she was going to come and take a swing at us… I thought for sure it was because of me. It was the sort of look I got in Akita all the time," said Yahiro.

He was worried that his cover had been blown in the faked kidnapping case and the group of culprits was coming after him for revenge. Or maybe he'd hurt the woman's family back in Akita, and she was out to get him for it.

But after he broke off from the others and realized the hostile feeling was gone, it occurred to him that either Yumasaki or Karisawa was the one in danger and decided to go back and check on them, threat of street attacks or not.

"In the past, someone who looked at me like that threw a Molotov cocktail…so it made me worry about them," Yahiro said.

"So basically, you just happened to catch the eye of that person by coincidence."

"Um, no? I was looking at everyone around me, so it was more like I found her…"

"Huh?" Himeka exclaimed, baffled.

"Well…I've been attacked in public all the time since I was a kid… so I developed a habit of looking at everyone I see, just to observe what they're like," Yahiro admitted casually.

"So when you're walking around, you're worried that every single person you pass might be an enemy?" she asked, aghast. "Does that mean you keep an eye out here on the roof, just in case someone comes up to attack us?"

"Yeah," he said.

Himeka exhaled heavily and grinned just a little bit. "You really are strange."

"You think so?"

"I do." She smiled gently.

"Oh… I guess I really am that weird."

Then Yahiro asked her thoughts about one more thing—about the combination of the hostility he felt while fighting against the street attacker and the joy he'd gotten out of the situation.

She heard him out until he was finished, and she didn't say anything for a while. She thought about it long and hard before replying, "Let's say that you killed me right now. Would you enjoy that?"

"No way."

"What about Kuon? Or all the other people on the roof you were watching out for?"

"I don't even want to imagine it," Yahiro replied earnestly.

"Then I think you're fine for now."

"Oh, okay."

"I'm not some psychology expert, but you have plenty of people you can talk to, so as long as you get it off your chest to someone else and don't hold those feelings inside forever, that alone should help change you, shouldn't it?"

Although her facial expression was flat, he could tell that she was taking his concerns quite seriously. Yahiro grinned slightly, acknowledging the warmth of her words.

"…That makes sense. Thanks. I'll try talking to Kuon about it, too."

"Ah, so you're finally on a first-name basis with him."

"Yeah. We talked it over," Yahiro explained, then found himself racked with concern for Kuon.

He said he was skipping school today to go to the dentist… I hope he's doing all right, he thought, worried that the injuries he personally inflicted might cause his friend to pass out again.

A park in Ikebukuro

As a matter of fact, Kuon *had* passed out.

But it wasn't because of Yahiro's punch.

He'd been hit by a completely different guy and laid out on the ground.

A few minutes earlier, Kuon was standing before Shizuo and his bandaged friend Tom, as they took a break in the park.

"Yo, Shizuo and…Tom, was it? I heard about your head wound."

"What? You're that Yahiro kid's friend, aren't you?" said Shizuo skeptically and gruffly.

Tom asked, "How did you know about my injury?"

"How could I not? I was the one who got the attacker worked up and led them to attack you," Kuon admitted, just like that.

Then he began to tell Shizuo all about what he'd done.

He bragged, gloated, even brought up Shizuo's brother, trying to get him mad.

And to no surprise, he succeeded at getting Shizuo to explode with fury.

And as Shizuo rounded on him, intent on violence, Kuon thought, *This is right. This is what I deserve.*

Horada had always been an adversary, so there was no need to apologize to him. He wasn't going *that* far to try to make himself a good person. But Tom didn't deserve what happened to him. Kuon decided that in order to settle that account, he needed to pay the proper price or else he wasn't worth his salt as a scheming mastermind. And he would certainly never surpass Izaya Orihara.

So this action required him to sacrifice himself.

If I die here...I'm sorry, Sis.

He envisioned his sister's face as Shizuo loomed.

And then Kuon ended up on the ground.

But it wasn't because he'd taken one of Shizuo's tremendous punches to the face.

It was because *Tom* interjected and socked Kuon in the face instead.

He'd taken one punch from Yahiro and now a twisting punch from above. Kuon hadn't been expecting it and couldn't even tense up before the force knocked him flat.

"Tom, why...?" gasped Shizuo.

"I'm the one who suffered because of him," Tom said. "So I hit him. Got a problem with that?"

This was not like the usual Tom. His gaze brooked no argument.

Shizuo understood his intention and let his anger dissipate. He shook his head.

"...No. No problem."

And back to the present.

"Why did you tell us? You could've stayed quiet, let it pass, and nothing would've come of it," said Tom, who couldn't understand Kuon's actions.

From the ground, he answered, "I got lectured by a very nosy urban legend, that's why... Would you believe that?"

Kuon wasn't lying, but he intended it to come off as confrontational. For whatever reason, he didn't feel like lying about his motivation, so instead he spoke of Yahiro as the "urban legend" Snake Hands, turning the truth into a challenge to be deciphered.

He expected them to consider his answer a joke and for Shizuo to explode with fury again—but the two debt collectors just looked at each other, then nodded with understanding.

Lastly, before he left, Shizuo said, "Fine. In honor of that urban legend, I'll let you go for today."

After they left, Kuon lay on the park ground, rubbing his cheek.

Ugh, that hurts... I think I might've broken another damn tooth... Although if Shizuo had hit me, I might actually have died...

"...Wha—?" Kuon abruptly realized why Tom had hit him. "Wait... was that Tom guy...protecting me?"

As a matter of fact, punching Kuon first, as Tom did, might have been the only way to defuse Shizuo in that situation.

In other words, the man had just saved the person responsible for his own injuries.

"Shit...dammit...dammit!"

He rolled his head back, covered his eyes with his arm, and felt shame at his own powerlessness.

Through bloodied lips, he admonished himself.

"This is why...I hate humanity."

♂♀

"Sorry about that, Tom."

"About what?"

"If I'd gone through with it, I wouldn't have been able to get away with saying, 'My bad.' Besides, the way he talked, it sounded like *Celty* told him to come here and fess up about what he did."

"Don't worry about it. I wanted to wrap that one up myself. Would have preferred to punch the goddamn street attacker myself, but I'll let the cops have that one," Tom said with a shrug. He scowled and balled his fist, staring at it. "It's been so long since I hit someone... I don't think I broke anything, but my hand sure hurts like hell."

Shizuo suggested, "Want to go visit him for help again? He can't do X-rays, though."

♂♀

Shinra's apartment—an hour later

When Celty returned, Shizuo and Tom were just leaving.

"Hey, Celty."

"Sh-Shizuo!"

Dammit! I wasn't ready for this encounter! Well, guess I just have to apologize...

She was getting ready to type her apology out when Shizuo bowed deeply to her.

"Thank you. Sounds like you were doing a lot for us behind the scenes."

Huh? She didn't know what he was talking about.

Tom added, "Honestly, I thought you'd have brought the guy to us all trussed up on a rope, but you convinced him to show up in person... That's impressive work."

Huh? Wha...? Eh?

"Well, we gotta get back to work. We'll find a way to show our appreciation some other time."

They patted the thoroughly confused Celty on the shoulder as they walked past, smiling gratefully, and returned to their office.

That left Celty standing in the entryway of the apartment, completely baffled.

What...? What's going on here?!

Had she simply lost a big chunk of her memory and not realized it?

The thought of being abducted by a UFO and having her memory tampered with left her feeling haggard and violated, and she rushed to Shinra for comfort...

But that is a story for another time.

NEXT PROLOGUE

Raira Academy—cafeteria

After the string of incidents, the developers of the *OPD* media franchise, WWW, made the following statement:

"We have no comment about the group of Dark Owls who appeared at the train station. But there is one thing we can say. Did someone cause this due to the influence of the Dark Owl? That might be possible. The Owl and the Dark Owl exist in every person's heart. They represent our good and wicked consciences, the angel and devil on each shoulder. But if someone gives in to the devil's temptation and kills another person, who says, 'We must crack down on the Bible'? *OPD* is not the Bible, just a simple work of entertainment. Please don't forget that."

Mairu Orihara read the comment on her smartphone, then said to Aoba with exasperation, "What you did ended up getting used as promotion for *OPD* after all, Aobacchi."

"Hmm...? Oh... Yeah, first the Underars claimed it was one of their art projects, so it was like the company swooped in from the top to scoop up the clout... And who told you about that?!" Aoba replied absentmindedly.

His lunch partners, Mairu and Kururi, rounded on him with complaints.

"Oh, come on! We heard it from Kuocchi! Look, all this stupid street attacker stuff means that people like us in the Always Walking Around in Animal-Themed Clothes Alliance get saddled with a bad reputation! And it turns out the group that was helping spread that stereotype is the Blue Squares? What gives?!"

"...Trouble..." [It's a pain.]

"S-sorry, sorry. Listen, I'll try to make it up to you by orchestrating something that will improve the image of those animal clothes you love so much," Aoba insisted. But on the inside, his mind was occupied with a different trouble.

He was thinking of a call he had with Yoshikiri the night in question.

"Hey, Yoshikiri. Nice job. Now I know just how strong Yahiro is."

"Huh?"

"I'll be honest—I didn't know you were that nimble. You might've been focused on avoiding getting hurt, but you managed to get real far against him. In fact, I'd say *you* could do pretty well against Shizuo Heiwajima, too, eh?"

"What are you talking about?"

"Uh...I'm saying...you were dressed as the street attacker so that you could ambush Yahiro, and I was filming it from afar. Then you ran up the roof and got away, right?"

"Huh? Didn't you get my text?"

"?"

"I totally sent you a message! I got lost, so I went back home and went to bed!"

After that, Aoba had gone back to his distant footage of the fight and examined it again. Indeed, the attacker fighting Yahiro seemed to be moving much too fast to be Yoshikiri. In fact, if Aoba were to be completely objective in appraising Yahiro's skill, his only conclusion was that Yoshikiri wouldn't stand a chance against him.

I was really hoping to have a video I could title "Snake Hands defeats the street attacker!"

It was only supposed to be a quick little cash grab for some spending money, but it left Aoba with a powerful disquiet in his chest.

As well as a keen, curious thrill.

So who the hell was that in the Dark Owl outfit?

♂♀

Rental office in Tokyo

In a small rental office within a commercial building, Shijima sat in the chair in the center of the room, his head still bandaged up.

But this time, it was not Earthworm standing at his side; it was a young man dressed in Dark Owl pajamas, the hood ripped near his mouth.

"So how was this Snake Hands fellow?" Shijima asked.

The man grinned. "Great, Mr. Shijima. He's tough, really tough!"

"I see. That was an expected benefit to monitoring the street attackers, then." He made it sound like he'd been watching *all* the attackers from the very start somehow.

"I wanted to observe what would happen to people who already had an extremist profile if I gave them a little chemical encouragement," Shijima continued. "But then things went the way they did before I could even use the drugs. How mysterious that people who were polar opposites ended up traveling the same path..."

The other fellow was tall but young enough that some might have still called him a boy. "They weren't opposites. They were all pieces of shit." He cackled.

"Yes...that's true," Shijima said. "Everyone's a piece of shit, including you and me."

"Right?" he said gleefully.

Shijima glanced down at his hands. He was holding a smartphone that was playing the video of the Dark Owl and Snake Hands fighting, but from a different angle than the video Aoba took.

"Say," he said, watching the Dark Owl on the video, "are you really human?"

"What does that mean? You ask like you know people who *aren't* human."

"That's because I do know a few. I've suffered on account of it. So what are you, Jami?"

"I'unno. Couldn't tell you myself. But..."

The boy named Jami grinned, his eyes glinting with a bestial ferocity.

He thought back on the urban legend dressed in shadow and the brief instant of pure murder that man had exhibited and flashed a youthful, wicked smile.

"I think maybe *he* could tell me the answer."

AFTERWORD

Next story preview!

A fishy new item has turned up at the antiques shop, Sonohara-dou. Kuon plans to buy and resell it for a hefty sum, but then a mysterious group shows up to snatch it! His hired transport, Celty, suffers a night of terror as a result. There are others lurking around, too, in search of quick money. What will happen to Celty? And what happens when the would-be villain Shijima finally makes a big move?!

Somehow, Yahiro ends up appearing in the minors' division of Rakuei Gym's Mixed-Species Martial Arts Tournament. Kuon tries to collect intel on the opponents so he can get some of the prize money, and Yahiro becomes a standout combatant without realizing it. Later on, Yahiro has to deal with a mysterious boy named Jami. Meanwhile, Kuon realizes that there's a mysterious group plotting behind the adult division of the tournament, which even Libei will compete in— and the group has its sights on Himeka and Shinra for some reason!

I might give you one of these two ideas, or I might do neither!

...I'm sorry. My plans aren't set in stone at all.

But whether I use one of these stories or something else entirely, I'm pretty sure the mysterious lad we just saw at the end of this volume will be involved. Hope you're looking forward to more life in the Headless Rider's Ikebukuro!

Anyway, hi, I'm Narita.

The in-universe story that appears in SHx3, *Owl of the Peeping Dead*, isn't based on any particular franchise. I just wanted to explore how scary it might be if you had people who went way too far, either as fans or as haters.

No matter the series, whenever fans get together offline and get really heated about stuff, whether malicious or not, I just hope that it doesn't turn into a scene of violence or nasty arguments.

Also, I'll admit that I invented this *Owl of the Peeping Dead* series and its live-action movie adaptation...and then I started getting jealous of it. So your punch line is that I'm the one who's experiencing the direst break from reality…

Please, folks, take care not to end up like me!

Now, at the point this book comes out in Japan, January 10, 2015, the new series of the *Durarara!!* anime will be airing!

Let me tell you, it's been such a long road since the plans for a second season were first hatched… I'm so overjoyed!

Also, it's going to be split into three cours, so there's a long way yet to go, even now that it's airing.

I've already done my supervising pass on the script for the final episode. I can tell you that parts that ran a little long in the original novels have been smartly compacted into a three-cour run that has a great dramatic tempo to it!

After seeing the anime staff in the production process, hearing the enthusiasm and effort in the voices of the actors during recording sessions, I thought ominously, *Oh, crap. This is good. It's going to be too good.* Durarara!!*'s entire image is going to get taken over by this anime!*

I still haven't seen the first episode, but I'm bursting with anticipation to experience the anime along with all of you!

And as the original creator, I've got to keep writing novels that live up to that anime at the very least, so I hope you check them out!

Also, on the twenty-ninth of this month in Japan, there's a new PS Vita game coming out, *Durarara!! Relay!* We've also got the *Durarara!! Re;Dollars* manga drawn by Aogiri in the pages of *G Fantasy*, along with other adaptations. Keep checking out the ever-expanding *Durarara!!* universe!

I've also got a bit of stuff to promote…

This month, I'm attempting my first ever "two books on one day" schedule with Dengeki Bunko!

I've got a spin-off of the *Fate* series called *Fate/strange Fake* coming out as a series with Dengeki Bunko, and it's out now, too! Please do check it out!

Lastly, my usual acknowledgments.

To my editors, Papio and Anami, and everyone at ASCII Media

Works and the printers, I'm sorry for making you put up with me for two books in a single month...

To the excellent folks who are bringing *Durarara!!* to life in different forms of media, including our new anime series.

To the family, friends, authors, and illustrators who support me.

To Suzuhito Yasuda, who manages to create such tirelessly wonderful illustrations for my books, despite being easily busier than me with his own career.

But most of all, to you all for picking up the continuation of *Durarara!! SH*.

Thank you, thank you all! I hope that we meet again soon!

November 2014—Ryohgo Narita